A VICTORY FOR THE PEOPLE

Long Elk ran, bending and twisting, while the mounted Head Splitter pursued him. Heads Off surged forward in a charge and this time his thrust was true. The enemy fell heavily in the mud and lay still.

Heads Off glanced quickly around. A Head Splitter was helping a wounded comrade swing up behind him. Beyond that, another enemy warrior kicked his horse around to retreat. All along the line of battle, the attackers were withdrawing. Several of the young Elk-dog warriors seemed inclined to pursue, but Heads Off called an end to the battle.

"Fall back!" he shouted.

He must not allow them to divide their slim force. They would be unprotected in open pursuit.

"We will have another chance," he reassured the returning young men.

THE ELK-DOG HERITAGE
THE SPANISH BIT SAGA   BOOK II

Bantam books by Don Coldsmith

The Spanish Bit Saga • Book I
TRAIL OF THE SPANISH BIT

The Spanish Bit Saga • Book II
THE ELK DOG HERITAGE

The
Elk-dog
Heritage

≫ ≫ ≫ ≫ ≫ ≫ ≫ ≫ ≫ ≫ ≫ ≫ ≫ ≫ ≫

DON COLDSMITH

BANTAM BOOKS
NEW YORK • TORONTO • LONDON • SYDNEY • AUCKLAND

*All of the characters in this book are fictitious, and any
resemblance to actual persons, living or dead,
is purely coincidental.*

RL 6, IL age 12 and up

*This low-priced Bantam Book
has been completely reset in a type face
designed for easy reading, and was printed
from new plates. It contains the complete
text of the original hard-cover edition.*
NOT ONE WORD HAS BEEN OMITTED.

THE ELK-DOG HERITAGE

*A Bantam Book / published by arrangement with
Doubleday & Company Inc.*

PRINTING HISTORY
*Doubleday edition published May 1982
Bantam edition / August 1987*

Published simultaneously in the United States and Canada

INTRODUCTION
BY ROBERT J. CONLEY
» » »

Anyone who has read *The Trail of the Spanish Bit*—the first book in Don Coldsmith's ongoing saga of his beloved Tallgrass Country of Kansas and of the people who inhabit and are a part of that land—has been eager to get on to the next installment, as have I.

Not too many years ago, American Indians, myself included, often commented that we were tired of seeing books written by white people about Indians. White people, we said, didn't understand our cultures. They had turned out hundreds of volumes filled with misinformation, books that continued to foster misunderstandings. We did not need more of them. Besides, there were a substantial number of good Native American writers begging to be published. Why not put their stories in print? In more recent years, most of us, I think, have modified that stance. We now simply want to see books that are written with understanding and sensitivity for the Indian cultures they are describing. Don Coldsmith's books are definitely of that high caliber.

I, for one, am pleased that Dr. Coldsmith has selected this subject matter for his own. He has a deep and abiding respect for Native American cultures and an understanding that rarely exists across cultural lines. He has a genuine sense of the mystic and the supernatural, without which no one can begin to understand the psyche of the American tribes. And he has a deep love and respect for the land—a strong and real sense of place. I have walked the hills of Don Coldsmith's Kansas with him and heard him speak of their beauty and life. I have watched and listened to him as he pointed out paths through the valleys and over the hills, paths where characters in his novels have run. Because these places were described in novels that I had read, the stories came alive for me again as I stood with their creator. The people, the land, and the spirits of each are alive and real to him, and he makes them live for us in his work.

In *The Elk-dog Heritage*, as Heads Off—the renamed Juan Garcia, one-time Spanish conquistador—becomes more assimilated into the lives and the culture of the People, we too are drawn more deeply into that world. But we see more than Juan Garcia's growing assimilation and gradual transformation into a respected chief of the People. We witness the evolution of a North American plains people from their "dog days" to their days of glory as horsemen of the plains; we see the birth of a warrior society; we watch the inner workings of a traditional tribal council in the nearly pure democracy of the plains hunting cultures; we see oral history in the making; and perhaps most significant of all, we see that, in spite of vast cultural differences between our contemporary society and that of the People, the People are, after all, but people.

The Elk-dog Heritage tells an exciting story—introducing us to new characters, while those we know from the previous novel continue to grow and develop—but it does much more than that. It presents another installment in a remarkably perceptive and detailed narrative of epic proportions. It delineates a dynamic culture, a civilization constantly and ingeniously adapting itself to new conditions, a people in transition (as all people always are)—a story without end.

Within the broad framework is played out the universal theme of the conflict between calm and reflective maturity on the one hand and restless, adventuresome youth on the other. In *The Trail of the Spanish Bit*, Juan Garcia became Heads Off. He introduced horses to the People, who called them elk-dogs, and he taught them horsemanship. Because of their newly acquired skills, the People were able, at long last, to win a decisive victory over their old enemies, the Head Splitters. In the past the People had always fought defensive actions against the Head Splitters. Now they suddenly had a new reputation as powerful horseback warriors.

The young men of the time of *The Elk-dog Heritage* (a few years have passed) are too young to have taken part in that famous fight. They have heard the story, and, of course, they share, in spirit, the sense of honor and pride that came to their people as a result of that victory—but they didn't take part in it. And now as young men (teenagers, really), they want their own share of glory. For ambitious, energetic youth, it is not enough to listen to tales of the past told by "old men." The young men must make their own mark, and they think they must make war in order to do so, even though the People have never been aggressive. Heads Off is faced with his toughest administrative problem, and in order to deal with it, he needs all of his own wisdom as well as that of his close friend and adviser, Coyote. The chief's power in this type of plains democracy is in direct proportion to his ability to persuade. Heads Off cannot simply order the young men to stay home and out of trouble.

As readers we can sympathize with both sides. The conflict is one we have all encountered. It crosses cultural boundaries and transcends time. The central problem in *The Elk-dog Heritage*, which is also the source of the novel's fascination and appeal, is how Heads Off, who is, after all, underneath his new identity still Juan Garcia, the Spaniard, will deal with this age-old dilemma within the context of the People's culture. It is at this point that Don Coldsmith's skill and perceptiveness reveal themselves to us from another angle. Heads Off is not the great white leader we have encountered in so much fiction, where the white man lost in the wilderness rises meteorically to fame, fortune, and leadership in an alien culture. Heads Off is not Tarzan of the Apes, nor is he the Man Called Horse (of the Hollywood film, not the original Dorothy Johnson story). He does not illustrate the "superiority" of the white man by out-Indianing the Indians. Heads Off needs the advice and the wisdom of Coyote in order to maintain the leadership position he has achieved—a position he was given, after all, primarily because he had a horse and a bit and skills as a horseman. Heads Off is a good leader, but he is only human, and that makes him all the more acceptable and believable.

Heads Off, like all the characters in this novel, like all in the Spanish Bit saga, is real. In *The Elk-dog Heritage*, the young have the faults of youth, and the old have both the wisdom and the folly of age. There are lessons here for all of us. And there's excitement, there's adventure, there's a good story told, and there is the promise of more to come as the tale of the People and of the Tallgrass Country continues to unfold in future volumes.

Sioux City, Iowa
November, 1986

Prologue
>> >> >>

In later years, in the tribal history of the People, it would be remembered that the split began immediately after the Great Battle. It was curious that this should be. The tribe had adapted to the changing culture which included the elk-dog. The hunting of buffalo was now so much easier that the People had become an affluent and respected group on the Plains.

And then, under the leadership of Heads Off, the young hair-faced outsider who had brought the first elk-dogs, the Southern band had met the dreaded Head Splitters in battle. For the first time in tribal memory they had not only stood fast before this enemy, but soundly defeated him. *Aiee*, the Great Battle would be retold in song for many generations!

The Southern band would henceforth be called the Elk-dog band, and Heads Off had reluctantly assumed the position of chief after the death of that leader in the battle. The Elk-dogs were now the most prestigious of the bands in the tribe. Their warriors' opinions were respected in the Big Council each summer at the Sun Dance. Their children were fat, and their women were happy. Their lodges were made of many skins, and each family owned increasing herds of elk-dogs.

So, it was a strange thing that at this time was to come the split that would nearly destroy the People from within. One would think that with the increasing wealth of the tribe, there could be no conflict. Yet it came to pass, in spite of the easy living that had become the expected norm.

Or, perhaps, because of it.

The People of earlier generations had been largely pre-occupied with survival. It was difficult to hunt the buffalo on foot, before the advent of the elk-dog. If hunting was poor, the winter would be hard, and there would be mourning for the dead among the lodges in the Moon of Hunger. It had been, as one elder noted, a time of many worn-out moccasins.

Now, with the elk-dog, the hunt was easier. There was more time in which to dream and plan, and to gamble and sing songs of bravery.

And unfortunately, there was more time for the young hotbloods, striving for warrior status, to boast and threaten and dream of combat with the Head Splitters. For many of the warriors of the People, the Great Battle had furnished more than enough combat for a lifetime. But there were those who had not been present, or had transferred allegiance to the Elk-dog band for prestige since the fight, who now yearned for further war. It was these restless souls who provided the breeze that fanned the sparks of trouble into open flames.

At first the split into two warrior societies was almost unnoticed. The age-old Warrior Society was entered at manhood when a youngster proved himself in the hunt or, more rarely, in combat usually defensive in nature.

Then came the elk-dogs, and those young hunters who were instructed in their use called themselves, jokingly at first, the Elk-dog Society. After the Great Battle, they had proudly assumed the name and its associated prestige.

Meanwhile the older warriors, those who had proudly fought beside their now fallen chief, began to refer to themselves as the Bowstring Society. In their pride of accomplishment they wished to make sure that the contribution of those who stood among the lodges and faced the charge on foot was not overlooked.

Thus, there were for a time two warrior societies, with mutual admiration and respect. The early Elk-dog men, in effect, belonged to both societies. Both groups rigidly adhered to the rules of the council. This was all as it should be, and would have continued indefinitely, perhaps, had it not been for the restless activity of the troublemakers.

The first inkling of a splinter group actually could be seen, in retrospect, before the Great Battle. A handful of young men had set forth on their own foray. They had encountered a large band of the enemy, who had ceremonially tortured, killed, and left the bodies of the youths to be discovered by the People. Still, this had seemed only an isolated incident. It was unlike the young men of the People to defy tribal custom to engage in a private foray of this sort. The problem was compounded by one fact above all else. Until this time, there had been no tribal custom that would govern the deliberate seeking of a fight with the Head Splitters.

1
>> >> >>

The old warrior watched as his nephews clumsily began to skin the antelope. He was uneasy, because they had drifted farther into the country of the enemy than he had intended. What had started as a pleasant hunt to teach the sons of his sister was now a threatening situation. He glanced apprehensively at the fringe of brush along the rimrock. The antelope had fallen in the worst area he could imagine. They must butcher rapidly and retreat to safer country.

He straightened to get a better look at the dangerous fringe of cover above them. Was that a trace of motion that he detected? How the old man wished that his eyes were as keen as when he was the age of the two youngsters before him.

Something plucked against his shirt like a thrown rock, and he glanced down in alarm. He was startled to see protruding from his chest the feathered end of an arrow. Still, his senses refused to accept its significance. A great feeling of weakness came over him and he sank to his knees, the pain of the blow finally reaching his consciousness.

The two youngsters looked around in alarm. He motioned for them to run, as three armed warriors sprang from the rocks on the hill and came bounding toward them. The younger boy dashed toward the horses, grabbing a dangling rein and swinging nimbly astride.

The other boy stayed just a moment too long at the side of his dying uncle. The other horses, alarmed by the sudden movements, leaped into a canter with their companion. The youngster still on foot made one futile grab at his horse's head. The rein burned through his fingers, and the horses were gone in a flurry of dust. He turned to face his attackers. He was unarmed, having laid aside his weapons to attend to the antelope. Even his skinning knife had been dropped in the excitement. He looked around. Not even a rock or a stick was available.

The three now surrounded him, young men little older than himself. One stepped forward and slapped him across the face with open palm. Counting honors by striking the enemy, he knew.

He had given up all hope of survival. The best he could hope for now was to die with dignity. Another of the enemy youths sprang and struck at him. He snatched at the other's weapon, but missed. Too bad, they would be more careful now. Vaguely, he wished that his captors would not feel it necessary to count too many honors today before getting on with it. It might be a very long day.

Heads Off, once Juan Garcia, son of a Spanish nobleman, sat comfortably before his lodge. He wriggled his shoulder against the willow backrest, and puffed slowly on the stone pipe. It was a beautiful spring day, and he was amused by the antics of his small son, Eagle, playing in the lodge doorway. Heads Off watched the lithe grace of his wife, the Tall One, as she moved efficiently around the fire, broiling a fat slab of hump ribs.

He could become easily aroused at any time by merely watching the lithe movements of her long body for a moment.

The girl glanced up at him and smiled, reading his thoughts. Their relationship had been a perfect one. Heads Off had never been aware of any marriage so meaningful in the far-off land of his birth.

He told himself that his reasons for remaining with the People were primarily based on accident—an injury, a pregnant mare which had been unable to travel, a broken lance point. Still, in the depths of his soul, he knew the truth. His primary reasons revolved around this slim girl and her family.

He could still scarcely believe that he had assumed the chieftainship of this band. There had been no leader surviving after the Great Battle, and the young warriors had asked him for leadership. Only with the help and counsel of his father-in-law, the Coyote, and the aging medicine man, White Buffalo, could he have accomplished it. And now, accepted in this position by the chiefs of the other bands in the Big Council, he had become more confident. Almost arrogant, if the truth were known.

He would long remember the manner in which his arrogance was shattered.

Hearing a commotion, Heads Off turned to look among the lodges at the edge of the camp. Three riders were approaching, singing and shouting and leading two more horses. His practiced horseman's eye immediately recognized that he had seen neither of the led horses before. This, even before he identified the riders.

The one in the lead was a cocky young man who had attracted his notice before. He had been sullen and inattentive during instruction sessions as a member of the Rabbit Society. Despite all his inattention, the boy had proved himself a passable horseman, though Heads Off despaired over his lack of discipline. What was his name, the chief tried to remember. The other boys had given him a nickname that had stuck. It had had to do with his unpleasant disposition. Ah, that was it! The youth was called the Badger. That animal was surly and aggressive, and the name fit very well.

Heads Off smiled at the appropriate way the People acquired their names. His own had been bestowed on him the first day he was found by the People. Sick and injured, he had removed his soldier's helmet, but to the observers he appeared to take off his head. The joke had been on the scouts of the People, but the name had stuck. Few probably remembered the origin of the name, but it now seemed perfectly appropriate to the former Juan Garcia.

Badger was closer now, and Heads Off could see that he was brandishing weapons above his head, shouting and singing as he rode.

An uneasy feeling of alarm nudged at the young chief's consciousness. He could not exactly identify the reason for his apprehension, but it was there. The irritating thing nagged at him like a festering thorn in a sore finger. What was it that was not quite right?

Coyote strolled over from his own lodge nearby, nodded to his son-in-law, and sat down. Heads Off could see that the older man's face also wore a look of concern. There was a definite feel of impending trouble in the air.

Badger was singing, a tuneless chant reciting deeds of valor. The two men could catch only part of the words.

"——have met the enemy and killed him——counted many honors——have blooded ourselves anew——."

Heads Off saw that across the foreheads of Badger and each of his two companions was a smear of blood. This was a ceremony sometimes employed to mark a young warrior's entry into manhood. A bit of blood from a youth's first buffalo kill was used to mark his face as a symbol of his success.

But, these young men had already been initiated into the warrior society. Why, then, the repeat ceremonial announcement?

Heads Off looked at the various weapons brandished by young Badger, and at the two unfamiliar horses the young men were leading. Reluctantly, still with the sinking feeling of dread, he was forced to acknowledge the meaning of their repeated blood ritual.

The youths had encountered one or two of the Head Splitters and had successfully defeated them. The blooding had been repeated as a sign of the first human kill by these youngsters.

The young chief was a bit puzzled as to why this troubled him. He, himself, had killed before. Perhaps he would again, if necessary. If necessary. Perhaps that was the key phrase. Still, there was something else.

"It is a bad thing, Heads Off." Coyote was speaking. "The young men must not go on private war parties without the consent of the chief and the council."

Of course. The young chief was so new to the position of authority that he had overlooked the crux of the problem. To act as these young men had done was to flout his authority.

Moreover, such thoughtless actions might easily bring danger to the People. To expose one's own band to the threat of a vengeance raid by the Head Splitters was unthinkable.

"You will call a council?" Coyote asked in a matter-of-fact tone. Heads Off never ceased to marvel at his father-in-law's ability to suggest and advise without seeming to do so. Of course, a council was the appropriate step. He nodded agreement, just as White Buffalo, the medicine man, strode through the camp toward them. The old man stopped, slightly winded from his brisk walk.

"You saw?" he demanded.

"Of course." It was Coyote who answered. "The chief will call a council for tonight to deal with this matter."

He motioned for the newcomer to be seated, and the three began to discuss the matter at hand.

2
>> >> >>

By full darkness, the appointed time for the council, the village was buzzing with excitement. Many of the younger of the People were elated, singing and dancing over the success of the young warriors. Actually, some of them appeared to feel that this council was to be held in honor of the incident. They certainly appeared to expect no reprimand.

The older, more mature members of the band were reserved and quiet, understanding the gravity of the situation.

In between were the young men of the Elk-dog Society. They appeared confused. They were young and exuberant, could easily understand the sentiments of the miscreants, perhaps even admire them. Still, their rigid training into the first disciplined mounted unit on the Plains made them resent this affront to authority.

Heads Off himself was not without mixed feelings. A few years earlier, he had been one of the miscreants in a faraway military academy. He could identify with the exuberant young hotheads. Perhaps this was the very reason he was determined to stop this rebellion against authority at the outset.

The council fire had been lighted and people were filing into the area to find good seats. There was still a happy, holiday atmosphere on the part of some of the exuberant young.

Coyote knew there were problems ahead, possibly worse than they had realized, when the young warriors arrived. The three in question were accompanied by several more budding warriors, and the entire group wore facial paint. The symbolism of the blooding ceremony was being extended. On the forehead of each member of the entire group was a broad slash of red paint.

Not that facial painting was uncommon. At the ceremonial dances the use of paint was sometimes quite ornate and spectacular. This was a different matter. This was not a ceremonial occasion. Here were young men, banding together as a group, and painted with the stark stripe of red. Unmistakably, this was intended to represent the drawing of blood. Coyote was afraid that it was also intended to represent a challenge to authority.

These things he communicated to his son-in-law as the People gathered for the council. Heads Off nodded, understanding the tension of the occasion. The ritual of council, however, was a pretty formalized thing.

The ceremonial pipe passed around the circle, each warrior blowing puffs of smoke to the four winds, to the earth and the sky. Finally, the pipe returned to the chief, and Coyote, acting as pipe bearer, restored it to its case.

Heads Off opened the council, asking for a report from the red-painted young warriors in the second row of the circle. Badger swaggered to his feet, while his followers gazed admiringly.

"My chief," he began, "we three were hunting." He indicated his two companions. "We came upon three Head Splitters. They were skinning an antelope, and did not even see us at first. I killed one with an arrow, one rode away, and one could not catch his horse. On that one we all counted several honors, before we finally killed. Then we blooded ourselves to honor the victory."

Heads Off nodded. The custom of counting honors had become familiar to him. To touch a live enemy was a great show of bravery, because of the danger involved. He had reservations as to the value of honors inflicted on a helpless enemy prisoner, but said nothing. One of the other warriors was asking permission to speak. Heads Off nodded.

"My chief," began the man, "I would ask these young men, had you thought what the one who ran away will tell? The Head Splitters may send a war party against us!"

"Let them!" sneered the Badger. "We will show them the worth of the People!"

The older warrior looked uncomfortable, but said nothing. Another man spoke.

"My chief, this is a dangerous thing. The People cannot go about in small groups looking for Head Splitters to kill."

Badger spoke, without permission.

"Those can who are not cowards!"

A murmur of shocked surprise at such a statement ran round the circle, followed by a smaller murmur of agreement with the speaker from his companions.

"Stop!" commanded Heads Off firmly. Why, he wondered momentarily, had he ever consented to this office? "There will be no such talk! There is no question of courage. Sees Far," he indicated the other warrior, "was with the bowmen at the Great Battle."

"Where were you, Badger?" the soft chuckling voice of Coyote interrupted.

Badger, of course, had not yet come of manhood two seasons ago at the time of the battle. Coyote knew this full well, but used the ruse to discredit the young warrior before the council. There was a general chuckle around the circle, and Badger shot a furious look at the speaker. Coyote shrugged innocently and said nothing.

Another of the Bowstrings spoke, after receiving the chief's nod.

"My chief, it seems the council should make some laws about this, as we do about hunting when the season is poor."

There were many nods of agreement, and a discussion followed. At length, the matter was resolved, though not to the satisfaction of the young dissenters.

Though not actually taboo, the undertaking of a war party was to be only with the knowledge of the chief and his advisers. To ensure this, they must have the vision of the medicine man, and his assurance of success. A war party of any size without this implied consent was to be considered in violation of the law.

The voting members of the council were in unanimous agreement on the new rules. There were those, however, who did not fail to note the sneers on the faces of some of the red-painted youths. They were sullen and silent, and Coyote doubted their cooperation.

One further matter was discussed, that of enforcement. It had always been the responsibility of the Warrior Society to enforce the law. Now, with more than one society, who would be the internal police force?

After much discussion, it was decided that the Bow-strings were to assume the function. They were the older, more stable group. Offenders were more likely to respect the age and experience of an older warrior than one of the young Elk-dog warriors.

It could easily be argued the other way, Heads Off thought uneasily. There was much to be said for social pressure from one's peers. Still, the problem seemed set-tled for now. He devoutly hoped that the sullen, with-drawn looks of anger on the red-smeared faces were temporary. He would not have wagered on it.

Coyote noticed with some apprehension another fact, as the council broke up. Several younger boys, not yet warriors, were hanging admiringly around those with the painted faces. To his great disappointment, he saw that one of these starry-eyed admirers was the son of Sees Far, one of those who had been called cowards.

No good could come of this.

3
》 》 《《

For some time it appeared that the young rebels had quieted and become cooperative. Badger and his friends were careful to ask the official ceremony of the medicine man before starting on a hunt. Apparently their medicine was good. They were successful at the hunting, and their lodges were well supplied.

The more moderate faction of the band began to relax somewhat. Even Heads Off hoped that these had been merely exuberant youths, who were now returning to the ways of their elders.

Coyote, however, still had a lingering, gnawing doubt. There were things which bothered him, and Coyote, above all, knew how to read people. Those of the People with little insight considered the little man an object of humor, a buffoon. The more perceptive of the tribe saw him for what he was. With his shrewd mind and wit, Coyote had always been respected by the chiefs in council. The disarming, chuckling little coyote-like laugh, which had earned him his name, could cover the most serious of manipulations in the politics of the tribe. As wise old

White Buffalo had once remarked, Coyote was able to lead without appearing to do so.

Just now he was disturbed about the young rebels. True, they seemed to be conforming, but there were questionable factors. All their hunts were with their own group. Of course, a man traditionally hunted with his friends. No harm in that. But *every* time? Coyote had noticed that the members of Badger's loosely organized group repeatedly turned down invitations to hunt with other hunters of the band. In fact, as time went on, the young followers of Badger seemed to become even more cohesive. Secretive, almost, thought Coyote. Yet they had broken no rules of the council. The precise dictum of the law was being obeyed, and no enforcement by the Bowstring Society was necessary.

There were annoying and worrisome things afoot, however. The members of Badger's group continued to blood themselves after every successful hunt. It became commonplace to see the young men returning from a buffalo hunt with faces smeared with crimson. Their songs of success were always loud and arrogant, full of boasting. Some people were referring to them as the "bloods" in a derogatory way.

Strangely, the group adopted this name for themselves. Just as their leader had taken for his own the disparaging term "badger," now his group took with pride the name "Blood Society."

Some of the elders of the band tried to convince themselves that here was a group of youths merely holding strongly to the proven ceremonial rituals of the ancestors. Coyote suspected more. He believed there was more ritual taking place, some of it in secret. The rebels had given up too easily. Their entire attitude was wrong. Instead of quiet obedience, there was this constant arrogance, a restless, ambitious self-esteem.

And then there were their dances. The Bloods celebrated after every hunt, even when there was little apparent cause. There were the songs and reenactment of the hunt, then dances recalling other hunts, and always the final act, the story of the controversial killing of the Head Splitters. The Bloods seemed to brandish this reenactment in the faces of the rest of the People. There was a certain defiance of authority in the reenactment of this event which had caused their censure.

Coyote must, he decided, talk to White Buffalo. Together, they could approach Heads Off if it appeared some action was necessary. It was unfortunate that the chief, with his upbringing far away, would not notice the subtleties of variant behavior such as this.

Coyote sauntered through the village toward the medicine man's lodge. He glanced toward the river, to the meadow where the youngsters of the Rabbit Society were receiving instruction. The warriors demonstrating the lessons were Standing Bird and Coyote's own son, Long Elk. He decided to watch for a while, turning aside from the path to walk to the meadow. Long Elk waved to him and came to meet him.

"No, no," insisted Coyote. "Go on."

Long Elk shook his head.

"We are nearly ready to stop," he said. "Wait for me a little."

The smaller children were practicing with throwing sticks or bow and arrow. Older youths on horseback were using the lance under Standing Bird's instruction. Coyote watched a young man make a good run at a willow hoop target, threading the circle neatly with his lance. It seemed such a short while since Coyote had first seen a buffalo killed in this manner. Heads Off had been a stranger then, and his control over the elk-dog seemed little short of a miracle. Now every young man of the People received instruction in the elk-dog medicine. *Aiee*, in other ways it now seemed that this had always been the way of the People.

Long Elk now dismissed his young charges and returned to where his father sat.

"Does it go well, my son?"

The young warrior squatted and shrugged.

"Well enough," he replied vaguely. Something was troubling him. Coyote remained silent.

"Father, did you know that some of the young men are taking instruction from Badger?"

This was no earthshaking news. The loosely organized educational system, the Rabbit Society, provided for instruction by almost any of the warriors who were so inclined. Most men spent some time with the children, where both boys and girls learned the use of weapons, and the athletic skills of running, jumping, and swimming.

Coyote waited, knowing he would hear more.

"Standing Bird and I believe Badger takes them on the hunt before they are ready."

If that were the only problem, thought Coyote. The entire matter was taking on a more ominous tone. If the impression of these young warriors was correct, then Badger might be actively seeking recruits for the Blood Society. The rebel group might be much more organized than he had thought. He must talk with White Buffalo.

Coyote visited a short while with the young men, and casually resumed his walk to the medicine man's lodge. He had not mentioned his suspicions.

White Buffalo was smoking in front of his lodge, and waved the invitation to sit. Coyote complied, and filled his own pipe. Crow Woman, the medicine man's wife, brought a burning twig to ignite the leafy mixture, and the two men smoked in silence for a time. They were friends of long standing, despite a considerable difference in ages. At one time White Buffalo had hoped that young Coyote might become his apprentice. He and Crow Woman had been unable to have children, so there was no son to carry on the position of medicine man. This had become a matter of considerable worry to him in recent seasons. None of the young men seemed interested. And, now there was this other matter, that of Badger. How could he voice his suspicions to Coyote?

In the end it was Coyote who broached the subject.

"Uncle," he began, using the People's term of respect for any adult male, "I would speak of the Bloods."

Surprised, the medicine man answered, "Yes, I, too."

They discussed their mutual fears and suspicions. There was really little to discuss, merely the uneasy feeling. For the medicine man, it was mostly a matter of reading attitude. Although the Bloods went through the ceremonial preparation for the hunt, their attitude was jocular and mocking. They were arrogant and insulting to the old medicine man, very demanding in their requests for the visions. So far he had been able to comply with their requests, but he wondered. What would happen on the day when he would have to advise against the hunt?

White Buffalo had also noticed another thing Coyote

had overlooked. At the dances in celebration of the hunt, there were women participating.

Warrior sisters! This too implied a well-organized warrior society. The young women of the society would remain celibate as long as they held status as warrior sisters, but could resign to marry at any time. It was a position of honor, requiring knowledge of the society's ceremonials and active participation in the rituals.

The alarming fact here was that if Badger's Blood Society had now included warrior sisters, it must have immense influence with the young people. The vows of a warrior sister were not to be taken lightly.

This added evidence of the prestige of the illicit warrior society was sobering to the two men. Though nothing definite had happened yet, they must make Heads Off aware of their observations.

They rose and walked toward the lodge of the chief.

4

>> >> >>

The two men found that their chief was not completely unaware of the undercurrents in the band. Though he might be a newcomer to the ageless customs of the People, Heads Off was a shrewd observer. He had sensed the tension behind the defiant attitude of the Blood Society. He had, in fact, discussed the matter at length with Tall One as they lay close in the warmth of their sleeping robes.

Coyote was much relieved to be able to share the burden of his knowledge, and the three men talked at great length. White Buffalo was convinced that a warning to Badger and his friends would be in order. Still, they had broken no rules. There was nothing to criticize. It was a matter of attitude. And, if one says his attitude is good, and he has broken no rules, who is to call him liar?

After discussion at great length, it was agreed that there was nothing to be done. In fact, the less talk the better. However, it would be important to watch carefully for any infractions or open defiance of the laws of the People.

The summer moved on, through the Moon of Thunder

and the Red Moon. It was nearly the Moon of Hunting before the next incident occurred.

Badger and a handful of the young Bloods were on one of their frequent hunts. These expeditions were not productive of much in the way of game. The young men did continue to ask the visions of White Buffalo before the hunt, but they were apparently ranging far and ignoring good hunting nearby. If they were hunting, Coyote thought grimly, it was not buffalo that they sought.

Thus, it was no great surprise when the small group of Bloods returned to the band after a three-day absence, without meat, but minus one horse. A severely wounded youth slumped behind one of the other riders, and still another showed minor injuries. One of the other horses limped from an arrow wound in the fleshy part of the hip.

Excitement rippled through the camp, and word of a council passed immediately. It was a foregone conclusion that the main purpose of the council would be to discipline the miscreants. Yet, despite this common knowledge, the Bloods continued to behave as if they were heroes.

From the standpoint of the chief, the council that evening was completely unsatisfactory. Neither Heads Off nor even the wily Coyote was able to entrap the young warriors into an admission that they had done anything wrong. They had merely been on a buffalo hunt, with approval of the medicine man. White Buffalo grudgingly acknowledged that this was true.

It was no fault of the innocent hunters, Badger insisted, that they had encountered a superior force of the enemy. They were lucky to escape with their lives. Still, Badger seemed to take far too much glory in the details of the fight. They had killed one of the Head Splitters and severely wounded another in the skirmish.

The council adjourned without action on the incident. There was none to take. The Bloods had still broken no rules of the council, and their account of the circumstances of the fight must be respected.

The Bloods immediately began a victory dance in celebration, much to the disgust of Heads Off.

Coyote was preoccupied with observing the ceremony. Someone had brought a drum and people began to gather as one of the girls tapped a rhythmic beat with the dogwood beater. The warriors of the Blood Society began the dance, stepping, singing, reenacting not only this but previous skirmishes with the enemy. Each had painted the now familiar broad band of crimson across his forehead.

The ceremony lasted nearly till dawn, and for Heads Off there was little sleep. He, as well as Coyote, had seen the looks of admiration on the faces of the younger boys. The children growing up must not be allowed to idolize these deviant young rebels. And, Heads Off thought in despair, there was so little that could be done about it. Even Coyote, who usually had suggestions, seemed at a loss. The thing was tearing the People apart. It was alienating father from son. Heads Off, as well as Coyote, had noticed as the council broke up, that the young son of Sees Far again followed the Bloods with an almost worshiping gaze. That honored warrior, in turn, seemed so filled with pent-up rage that it appeared for a moment that he would physically attack Badger. How can a man react when he sees his son following the wrong path?

At least, Heads Off thought to himself as he turned restlessly on his robes, the boy is not quite old enough to ride with the Bloods. Maybe something will happen for the best. He did not actually believe it.

Toward morning, the distant thump of the drum was becoming tired and slow. The diminishing vigor of the song was replaced by another sound from a distant part of the camp.

It started as a low wail, rising in volume and pitch, moaning and grating on the ear of the listener as it grew. Heads Off recognized the sound, although he would have preferred to ignore it. The unnerving wail was the Mourning Song of the People. It came from the far side of the encampment, and the chief knew without investigating from whose lodge it came.

Bird Woman had been widowed in the Great Battle. With the help of her brother, Sees Far, she had maintained her lodge as Fox Walking, her oldest son, came of age. She had staked her entire future on the young man, and many had been distressed when he had followed Badger and the Bloods. Now he had been severely wounded in the skirmish of the day. The wail from the distant lodge could mean only one thing. Fox Walking was dead.

Heads Off turned miserably, frustrated at his inability to take any action. Tall One placed a comforting arm across his chest and snuggled close, wanting to help, but equally frustrated. The girl did not fully realize how very important her mere presence was to the troubled young chief.

5
>> >> >>

Some relief from the internal pressures of the band was provided by the annual move into winter camp. Heads Off was thankful for any distraction at this time.

Stone Breaker, the weapons maker, had requested that they move by way of the flint quarry. They could replenish supplies of the scarce commodity, and still move into the desirable area for wintering before the Moon of Falling Leaves. The suggestion seemed a good one. Within three suns the Elk-dog band was on the move.

The chief was concerned about the attitude of Sees Far. That warrior was brooding, with a black sullen hate, over the death of his nephew. He had forbidden his son, Yellow Bird, to associate with Badger and the Blood Society. This naturally resulted in defiance on the part of the boy. The entire band was aware that the youngster still covertly followed the Bloods.

Heads Off again discussed the possibilities with Coyote, and neither saw a solution.

"It is like the river where it comes near the falls," Coyote said grimly. "The water moves slowly at first, then faster and faster."

The young chief nodded grimly, agreeing with the analogy. Unfortunately, there was an unspoken extension of the same mental picture. The water must inescapably be pulled over the edge, to fall crashing on the rocks below.

The temporary stop at the flint quarry was profitable. Near the head of a sheltered pocket in the rolling prairie was an outcrop of white stone. The entire area was dotted with ledges and protrusions of this sort, jutting horizontally from the lush green hillsides. On the surface of these stones could often be seen the outlines of small aquatic creatures, snails, and water plants. These fossil impressions in the limestone were a matter of curiosity to the People, but the valuable significance was of a more practical nature. Here and there, sheltered by overhanging white stone, were veins of hard blue-gray flint. Some of the better quarries had been worked for centuries. At the site now visited by the People, the horizontal layer of the precious stone was only a hand's span in thickness. Its breadth and depth were unknown, but a deep layer of rejected chips shifted underfoot as one approached the place. The vein of flint had been used by many tribes for many generations.

Stone Breaker squatted in the indentation of the hillside and methodically knocked flakes of the material loose with a large rock. Some of the warriors, taking pride in their own ability, joined the craftsman and gathered flints for their own use, or asked his expert advice. Stone Breaker, though lame from an old injury, was the acknowledged authority in weaponry. His skill was recognized among the other bands of the tribe, and a spear point made by Stone Breaker was highly prized among the People.

Still, Heads Off was anxious to lose no time here. The quarry was used by many tribes, including the Head Splitters. It would be well to move on as soon as practical into winter camp. Consequently, after a few suns, the young chief announced the move.

By the time Sun Boy had carried his torch halfway up the sky, the People were traveling south. They would winter, Heads Off decided, in the same general area where he had spent the first winter with the People. How long ago it seemed now. He had been lost and injured, and Coyote had quietly seen to his needs, taking him into his own lodge as the winter approached. Now, returning to the same area seemed like going home. And, he reflected, how simple things were then. His major problem was to return to his own people. He had fretted impatiently at every delay, reacting irritably and miserably. At the time he had considered that season one of misery and frustration.

Now it seemed in memory, a pleasant, uncomplicated time when things were straightforward and all problems had simple answers. Compared to his present situation, the answers had been simple. Now, he must deal with all the friction of the internal politics of the People. In addition, he now carried the responsibility of a family man. His son, Eagle, had already taken part in the ceremony of the First Dance. Soon, there would be another child in his lodge. Tall One was just beginning to show the telltale change in shape, and the slightly different swing to her walk. Heads Off smiled to himself. Thoughts of Tall One always made him feel good.

This reverie was rudely interrupted by the approach of a scout. Standing Bird loped up and slid his mount to a stop, almost touching the chief's gray mare.

"My chief, there are people ahead. Head Splitters."

"A hunting party?"

"No, no, they have women and children with them, and carry their belongings."

Heads Off relaxed somewhat. There would likely be no trouble. Neither group would initiate conflict, since there would be too much danger to the families of the warriors.

"It is good. Pass the word. We will move slowly ahead until we sight the other party. If you find Sees Far, send him to me. Then you return, too."

Standing Bird kneed his horse into a fast walk and started on toward the rear of the column. Heads Off lightly touched the little mare's flank and moved toward the front.

The confrontation took place in a broad, open meadow. Both groups desired it so. As soon as the other group was in view, the People drew together in a tight knot, women and children in the center. Around this nucleus clustered the baggage animals and loose horses. The perimeter was ringed by mounted warriors, quietly circling, ready for any eventuality. The other group, at a few hundred paces, was carrying out a similar ritual.

Three riders emerged from the other band and approached at a walk. Heads Off glanced around. Everything was in readiness.

"Badger," he called, "you will make no move of any kind!"

"Of course, my chief." The other smiled sarcastically.

Heads Off, flanked by Sees Far and Standing Bird, rode slowly forward to meet the strangers. Observing the ritual, the approaching strangers stopped halfway between the two groups and waited. Heads Off and his cortege cautiously rode to a conversational distance and reined their horses to a stop. Beyond the mounted Head Splitters, he could see at the far side of the meadow the women and children of the enemy group as they huddled together. Warriors circled protectively, as in his own band.

The other chief raised a hand in greeting, using both the spoken and sign languages. Heads Off spoke none of the other's tongue, but the sign talk was universal. He returned the greeting.

There followed diplomatic small talk of the weather and hunting. Heads Off stated that the People had just come from the flint quarry, where they had replenished their supply of the stone.

"Yes, you will need many weapons," retorted the other smugly. "Your young men have much to learn."

The emissaries of the People gripped weapons hard, but made no move. Any reply was up to their chief. Heads Off, his calm exterior belying his tension, glanced at Sees Far. It was only to be hoped that that warrior, with his recent family tragedy, could control his emotions. If he were to strike out in anger, a bloody conflict would follow. Sees Far appeared calm and under control. He was a methodical thinker, and the gravity of the moment was clear to him. After all, thought Heads Off grimly, the object of the wrath of Sees Far was actually more within his own band than with the enemy. What a strange situation.

"My chief," he signed in answer to the other, "*all* men have much to learn." There was only a trace of a veiled threat.

The wrinkles around the eyes of the enemy chief tightened just a trifle, and he smiled a hard smile. He had heard of this hair-faced chief of the People, and recognized him by reputation. A calm-appearing but a dangerous man, it was said. This would be a good point to terminate the meeting.

"So be it," he signed briefly, "until we meet again!" He turned his horse, exposing his back to the young hair-face with perfect confidence, and rode slowly back toward his own band.

The People did likewise, and the two groups circled each other warily and parted, continuing their respective directions.

6
>> >> >>

Hunting was good, with warm days and cool nights, and the People prepared much dried meat for the winter. Some was pounded fine, mixed with melted suet, nuts, and berries, and stored in lengths of buffalo intestine in sausage-like rolls.

Many robes were cured, and skins tanned for the making of garments. During the long warm days of the Moon of Falling Leaves the People prepared the lodges for winter. In the space behind the skin lining of each lodge, normally used for storage, armfuls of dry grass were stuffed as protection against the onslaught of Cold Maker.

It was a busy time. Even the troublemakers were occupied with hunting and storage of provisions, and the disquiet subsided somewhat. Thus there was a respite from stress within the band. It began to appear that the potential for trouble was lessening. Heads Off was afraid, however, that this was misleading. He knew, and Coyote verified, that the mild weather of the following spring would make the young men restless. Then would come the time of trouble, as they began to flex young muscles in the Moon of Greening Grass. The chief hoped that he would be able to create enough diversion to prevent any major incidents. Perhaps, even, to keep the band moving without permanent camp until after the Sun Dance in the Moon of Roses. That might be worth a try.

But for now, Sun Boy's torch grew weaker, and his daily run across the sky grew shorter. Long lines of geese honked their way across the sky, heading for southern waters. Heads Off stood and watched, longing to follow, yet remaining by choice. His longing for his warm lodge and loving wife was far greater. He placed an arm around her enlarging waist, and Tall One leaned her head on his shoulder. Since their marriage, now three seasons old, they had loved the sharing of sights and sounds. The honk of the geese in the fading evening sky, the scent of nature's time of ripening, recalled for both the long sunny days of their first weeks together. That, too, had been in the Moon of Falling Leaves. This and the natural beauty of the season had made it his favorite of all moons of the year.

The spectacular gold and purple of the autumn flowers, the muted reds and yellows of the tall prairie grasses, faded before the arrival of Cold Maker. There were a few storms that howled and whistled around the warm lodges, but on the whole, it was a mild and open winter. At no time was there snow on the ground for more than a few days before Sun Boy again wrestled the Cold Maker back toward his northern domain. Coyote chuckled, pleased at the repeated victories of Sun Boy. *Aiee*, not always were the People so fortunate!

Heads Off, during long evenings of sharing a social smoke with his father-in-law, also shared his thoughts. Would it be possible to keep the band moving to provide a distraction for the Bloods?

Coyote puffed slowly, exhaled the pungent blue smoke, and watched it curl toward the smoke hole at the apex of the lodge. He nodded.

"This may be a good thing, Heads Off. It could do no harm. The moving would be much work, but might distract the young warriors." He puffed again, and nodded to himself. "It might at least keep things quiet until we arrive at the Sun Dance. Then that will keep them busy for a while."

"I had also wondered," continued Heads Off, "if it

might be well to lead a raid on the Head Splitters, to let the Bloods have their fill of fighting."

"I think not, Heads Off." Coyote shook his head thoughtfully. Until the arrival of the elk-dogs, the People had not been fighters. Their defense was that of run-and-hide. Ever since the success of the few contacts with the enemy in recent years, it was difficult to break out of the old pattern. Coyote still thought in terms of avoiding trouble wherever possible. "Why," he continued, "should we look for danger when there is none?"

Heads Off was forced to agree. To lead a raid would only be to sanction the type of action they disapproved of by the Bloods. He nodded. "It was only a thought," he said absently. Every possible answer to the problem in the band must be considered.

White Buffalo was taken into confidence and the plan was outlined. The old man nodded eagerly. He could be of great help. His was the decision when to fire the dry prairie in the spring, to hasten the greening and bring the buffalo back. He could appear to make an error, decide for the burn too early, and the greening would not come. Then it would be necessary to move again. The three plotters talked long, planning each step carefully.

Tall One and her mother, Big Footed Woman, interjected an idea into the conversation. A few carefully selected women could help. It would be a simple matter to complain about the campsite, the water, fuel supplies, even the quality of the available game. With enough complaints, the chief would have no alternative but to order another move.

The men were delighted.

"But, only a few women," Coyote cautioned. "They should not even tell their husbands of the plan."

It was agreed that even these women were to know as little as possible of the entire scheme. They would merely be encouraged to talk discontent to their husbands and neighbors. This would provide yet another distraction from the potentially serious matter at hand.

Antelope Woman, wife of Standing Bird and best friend of Tall One, was the only woman taken into full confidence. These three women assured the chief that they could foment enough trouble when the time came.

White Buffalo ordered the firing of the grass so early in

the Moon of Greening that the first blades of grass had
not yet appeared. Some of the elders of the band shook
their heads and clucked their tongues. The mistake was
apparent to them. *Aiee*, White Buffalo must be too old
for his position, they told each other.

The People waited, and there was no greening. The
medicine man had chosen his time well. It became so
depressing to look at the blackened prairie that the band
began to grumble, and the chief ordered the move to a
better area. At least, there would be dry grass for the
horses. The band filed over the low range of hills, their
innumerable dogs trotting alongside.

In the next area, the medicine man chose perfectly the
time for burning, and the grass began to green in a few
days. But, no buffalo came. There were an occasional
animal or two, enough to provide meat, but the expected
big herds did not materialize. No one really suffered.
Only a few even resorted to eating their dogs, and some
of these did so by preference.

The men were kept busy by the need to hunt, however, and the dissidents were too preoccupied to make
trouble. White Buffalo was willing to take credit for the
success of the entire affair, but there was a great deal of
luck involved, too.

When the Bloods began to grow restless, it was considered time for the women to begin their complaints. It
began at the watering place. Making sure there were
other women nearby, Tall One and Antelope Woman
carried on a lengthy exchange about the murkiness of the
water. It was crystal clear, but by the time they left, the
women who overheard were questioning the contents of
their own waterskins. Rumor swept through the camp
that the water was bad.

As one final event, Tall One staged a complaint to her
husband in the presence of several of the People. She
berated him for choosing a campsite where there was
little fuel and scarce game, of poor quality. Though the
entire thing was preplanned, Heads Off was hurt badly
enough by the tirade that he did not have to pretend to
any great extent when he stalked away in a huff. No
matter, thought the girl. She could make it up to him
later. She had found it surprisingly difficult to publicly
embarrass her husband, even for good cause.

Two of the older Bowstrings who had overheard the tirade stood chuckling as Tall One flounced past.

"*Aiee*," one remarked to his companion, "our chief carries a heavy burden."

Tall One realized that the jest was intended for her ears. She was unsure whether it was to refer to her expansive waistline, or to her temperament, but she must act her assumed role for the present. She wheeled and strode over to the pair.

"My husband's heaviest burden," she snapped, "is that he leads warriors such as you two!"

She turned and marched off. The men chuckled, pleased. A woman with spirit was prized by the People. Their eyes, as they watched the retreating form, said that they did not consider the chief's burden heavy at all.

7

The move took place next day, without even a warning. Word passed that because of the scarcity of game, the band would work slowly northward, and hunt as they traveled. In this way, they would arrive at the Sun Dance with the rest of the tribe. It would do no harm to arrive a bit early. It was unlikely that the Bloods would leave the festivities once they had arrived.

The location for the Sun Dance, agreed upon the previous year, would be on the north fork of Walnut River. It was a favorite site for this most important annual event of the People.

The strategy outlined by the chief and his advisers worked well. A different camp was established every two or three days. White Buffalo directed their journey in a zigzag fashion, taking many more suns than would have been actually necessary. The wily old medicine man was successful in the finding of buffalo in most cases, so that his devious winding route was not suspected by the dissidents.

The warriors continued to be moderately successful at

the hunt, and gradually the band drew nearer the site of
the Sun Dance.

The Elk-dog band was not the first to arrive. By custom, the immediate family of the Real-chief of the tribe
was responsible for the site, the dance arena, and preparations. Therefore, the Northern band under Many Robes
had arrived first and begun the construction of the Sun
Dance arbor. Poles had been lashed together to form the
framework of the open-sided structure, and men were
handing armfuls of leafy brush to form a shady roof for
the week-long events.

The young men of the newly arrived Elk-dogs staged a
mock charge, wheeling their horses and whooping in a
grand celebration. Some of the Northern band joined in
the festivities, and the combined forces circled the camp,
shouting and singing and brandishing weapons.

Heads Off was tempted to join the display. His young
blood was stirred by the colorful spectacle, but he somehow felt that it might not be appropriate for the dignity
of his office.

The young chief noticed that many of the warriors of
his own band were not participating in the exuberant
arrival celebration. Most of the Bowstrings, but also some
of the Elk-dog warriors were merely watching, some with
stern looks of disapproval. He glanced around and noticed Sees Far, sitting on his bay mare. The man was
glaring at the proceedings with such a hostile gaze that
Heads Off was again deeply concerned. He had never
seen an individual change so rapidly.

Sees Far had been a quiet, easygoing man, well-liked
and competent in his skills. He was by far the best scout
and tracker in the entire band, but very modest about it.
The band had relied heavily on his abilities in more than
one encounter with the Head Splitters. Now, since the
death of his nephew and the interest of his own son in
the Bloods, Sees Far had changed. He was moody, grumpy,
and almost irrational at times. Former friends had begun
to avoid him because of his unpleasantness.

Heads Off was deeply concerned lest the skills of Sees
Far be lost at a time they might be most needed. He
could understand how a man with family problems might
become so preoccupied that he would be unaware of all
else. Even now, Sees Far sat alone, without friends.

Damn that stupid, arrogant Badger and his cursed Blood Society, thought the chief. He kneed his horse around, intending to approach Sees Far for a friendly conversation, but the other rode slowly away, not looking back. The very slope of his shoulders indicated his utter desolation. The chief abandoned his intention.

Instead, he turned and rode through the camp to pay his respects to the Real-chief. He waved and nodded to friends and acquaintances of the Northern band as he passed. The camp was well laid out, he observed. Old Many Robes had been an able chief for many seasons. The grass and water were good. Areas for each band's campsite were level and clear. By age-old custom, the bands camped in a traditional pattern around the central Dance Lodge. Each band occupied the same relative position in the circle as the seat of its chief in the Big Council.

Thus, the camp of the Northern band was already established to the north of the Dance Lodge. The Elk-dogs, being the Southern band, would establish camp on the opposite side. Next on their left would be the Red Rocks, followed by the Mountain band. The Eastern band would occupy the northeast segment of the circle. A space was always left directly to the east, as a doorway for Sun Boy after his rising.

None of the other bands had yet arrived, Heads Off noted. A group of excited young horsemen swept past, singing and shouting, and young women paused to wave and call a greeting. Everyone was being caught up in the excitement of the festive occasion. Heads Off had always been impressed, since he first witnessed the Sun Dance, at the resemblance to a country fair in his own homeland far away. There was excitement in the air, a carnival atmosphere. There would be family reunions, dances of both ceremonial and social nature, feasting, telling of stories, and of course, the Big Council. Each chief would report the events of the year for his band. Thinking this sobering thought, he became depressed again.

Heads Off had nearly reached the lodge of the Real-chief when another cluster of horsemen clattered past. He glanced up, and was startled to see Badger and his companions painted with the ceremonial stripe of scarlet across their brows. This was a complete departure from tradition. Even Heads Off, though a relative newcomer to the tribe, was aware that he had never seen ceremonial painting done merely to greet one's friends and relatives at the big camp. The now familiar uneasy feeling of dread gnawed at his stomach for a moment.

The gray mare stopped before a resplendent lodge of nearly thirty skins, and Heads Off called a greeting.

"*Ah-koh*, my chief! I am Heads Off, of the Southern band."

The Real-chief himself appeared at the doorway, and beckoned the visitor inside.

"*Ah-koh*, my friend! Come and smoke."

A young man stepped forward and took the reins of the mare, leading the animal to grass and water. Heads Off stooped and entered the lodge.

His host led the way around the cooking fire to the pile of robes opposite the doorway. He motioned the younger man to a seat, and a woman brought a pipe and filled it. Heads Off brought forth his own pipe, and the two lighted their respective instruments with a stick brought from the fire by one of the wives of the host.

The skirt of the lodge had been raised a few handspans on the south, and a comfortable breeze made the place quite appealing to a hot dusty traveler. The two men visited, talking of the weather, the mild winter, the hunt, and the lack of any contact with the Head Splitters. Then the old chief suddenly leaned forward confidentially and spoke on a new subject.

"You have trouble with some of your young men?"

Heads Off was astonished. He had long since become aware that the old chief was an extremely acute observer. The Real-chief also undoubtedly had observers to report to him. But how, only moments after their arrival, had he known of the internal politics of one of the bands under his jurisdiction? Once again, Heads Off marveled at the astuteness of the old man. Truly, he was a chief.

8

>> >> >>

Little was accomplished in the ensuing conversation. Heads Off informed the Real-chief of the sequence of events, while the other nodded understandingly.

"This has happened before, Heads Off. The young men wish to have their own warrior society. They always grow up and return to the ways of the People."

"But, my chief, they have had encounters with the Head Splitters, and have been successful."

"That is the bad part," agreed old Many Robes. "They do not remember what happened to the four at Sycamore Creek." He shook his head. "*Aiee*, some day they will meet a stronger force, and their learning will be a hard lesson."

In conclusion, the old chief agreed that there was little to be done. The Bloods should be ignored as much as possible, unless they broke rules of the council. The two agreed that in the Big Council, Heads Off would make no mention of the young dissidents. He would report on the movements of his band, but minimize the role of the Bloods and their skirmishes.

Heads Off also described the subterfuge that had been

used to keep the band moving. The Real-chief chuckled at the part played by the women. *Aiee*, he thought, if any can handle this problem, it is the Elk-dog band!

The young chief left the lodge of Many Robes feeling somewhat better. To be sure, the situation was unchanged, but now his responsibility was shared by another, an authority figure. It helped immeasurably, simply to feel that the Real-chief understood the situation.

Heads Off retrieved his mare, nodded thanks to the young man who handed him the reins, and swung to her back. He skirted the site of the Sun Dance, and arrived at the camp of the Elk-dog band. Pole skeletons for the lodges were tilting against the sky, and women called to each other as they established their lodge sites. The children ran excitedly in and out, accompanied by yapping dogs. Heads Off threaded his way among the lodges in various stages of construction, and located his family.

Coyote and Long Elk had assisted in placing and tying the poles, and were just raising the skin cover into position on the lodge of Heads Off. Tall One stood a bit aside, her near-complete pregnancy preventing the strenuous effort required to lift the heavy cover. The young chief stepped down and took a place alongside Big Footed Woman to assist in the lifting. Their combined strength swung the lifting pole, and the lodge cover, nearly thirty skins in size, settled into place. The women circled the lodge frame, dragging and smoothing the cover as they pulled it into position.

The men, meanwhile, turned to the slightly smaller lodge frame alongside, that of Coyote's family. By the time the women had laced the front of the lodge of Heads Off and positioned the smoke flaps, they had erected the skin cover on the other structure.

As they strained to lift it into place, a young woman passed and smiled covertly at Long Elk. That young man became embarrassed and confused, and nearly lost his hold on the lifting pole.

"*Aiee*," Heads Off chided his brother-in-law, "we will soon be lifting a new lodge for Long Elk!"

The women joined them and completed the positioning of the lodge cover. In a short while, cooking fires were crackling, and the children of Coyote and Big Footed Woman were bringing firewood and buffalo chips for fuel.

The men settled for a smoke against their willow backrests. The establishment of a new camp was always a satisfying time, reflected Heads Off. The site was clean and without the odor it would have later. Everyone was tired, but satisfied and happy that the journey was over.

In addition, this time held other advantages. It was the first site for many suns where the band had erected the big skin lodges. While on the move, the temporary camps were established with only crude brush shelters or in the open; it was far too complicated to set up the lodges for only a night or two. Now, setting up the more permanent camp seemed like coming home, Heads Off thought.

The other pleasant aspect, of course, was that this camp would include all the excitement and revelry of the Sun Dance.

Sun Boy carried his torch slowly toward the western edge of the world, and Heads Off began to relax. Tall One brought meat, and sat beside him to eat. Young Eagle, tired from all the excitement of the day, played sleepily before the new lodge and accepted bites of food from his parents as they ate. Finally, Tall One rose and packed the youngster off to his sleeping robes. Then she returned to sit beside her husband as he smoked, leaning against his knees.

"You spoke with the Real-chief?"

He nodded. "There was not much to say. Many Robes sees the matter well."

"What will he do?"

"Nothing. He can do nothing, unless the Bloods break the rules of council or the laws of the People."

Tall One nodded. The same old story.

"I will say very little of the thing at the Big Council," her husband continued. "That will hurt the Bloods most of all."

"That is good, Heads Off. They take themselves much too seriously now."

The lengthening shadows brought a chill to the prairie, and she crept closer to him for warmth. Finally she rose, to seek the shelter of the lodge and the soft comfort of their sleeping robes. Heads Off followed. Let tomorrow take care of itself. For now, he was at home, secure in the arms of Tall One.

Next day the Mountain band arrived, led by Black

Beaver. The wheeling and shouting of the mock charge
was repeated, and the newcomers were joined by the
Blood Society in full force, their faces again ceremonially
painted. Again, Heads Off became anxious. People were
accepting this group of upstarts all too readily.

The celebration quieted in due course, only to be repeated three suns later when White Bear led the Red
Rocks band in from the southwest. There had been much
intermarriage with the Red Rocks after wintering together two seasons ago, and there were many joyous
family reunions and friendly greetings.

Meanwhile, Heads Off knew, the gossip and rumor of
the camp would have been spreading like prairie fire.
Everyone would have heard the story of the Blood Society by the time of the Big Council.

It was several suns before the last of the bands arrived,
the Eastern band under Small Ears. The Eastern band had
for many years had a reputation as non-conformists. Their
chosen territory was somewhat different in topography
than that of the other bands. They spent more time in
the wooded areas along the larger rivers, leading to a
slightly different life style. In addition, their chief, Small
Ears, had a tendency to glory in the differences, and
regard them as unique advantages of his band.

The rest of the People regarded the Eastern band with
good-natured amusement. There were jokes, Heads Off
had learned, built around the reputation of that group
and its oddities.

One of the Elk-dog warriors had once come walking
back from a hunt, without game, Heads Off recalled, and
with his bow broken in the fall which also had lost him
his horse. The other men had chuckled and chided him
for his ineptness.

"*Aiee,*" exclaimed the man's wife. "What am I to do
with him? His grandmother was of the Eastern band."

General laughter had followed.

Now, the Eastern band had arrived, and the medicine
men began the daily circuits of the camp, singing the
announcement of the Sun Dance, to begin four suns
hence. The Sun Dance itself would last seven days, a
non-stop celebration. As dancers became tired, their places
would be taken by others, and after food and rest, they
would return.

The major theme was the return of the sun, the grass, and the buffalo after a long winter. There would be songs of thanksgiving, of patriotism, and songs of hope for good health. People with infirmities would dance and offer sacrifices, with entreaties for healing.

Preparations continued after the four suns of announcement were begun. The family of Many Robes had killed a huge buffalo bull. The skin and intact head were carefully arranged at the west end of the dance arbor over a brush form. The resulting effigy would be the focal point of the festivities for the coming days.

But, before the first ceremony of the Sun Dance, before any of the important activities of the festival, there was one other necessary step. The first day of announcement, begun after the arrival of the Eastern band, was also the signal for the official gathering of the tribe on the first evening. As Sun Boy carried his torch toward earth's rim, the People began to gather for the Big Council.

9

>> >> >>

The Big Council would be held, not within the Sun
Dance structure, but adjacent to it. A fire had been lighted
as the shadows lengthened, and fuel stacked nearby to
replenish the flames.

The fire was certainly not needed for warmth. The
evening was hot and still, and the cooling breeze of the
prairie had not yet begun to bring the customary chill to
the lengthening shadows of evening. Yet a fire was essen-
tial to council. Somehow the mystique that surrounded
the ceremonial fire was part of the ritual involved. Certainly, nothing so important as the Big Council could be
held without the solemn effect of the council fire.

Some people arrived early, to be sure of a good place in
the circle. Each band was limited to the traditionally
assigned arc, with the Northern band occupying that
segment, and the others in relation to it, exactly as in
their campsites. This arrangement was never discussed,
merely practiced. The origins of the custom had been
lost in antiquity. It had always been so.

The chiefs of each band would sit closest to the ritual
fire. Directly behind were the sub-chiefs and principal

warriors of each band. An occasional woman would be
found in the second rank, and it was not unusual for
women to speak in council. This had been a thing of
great wonder to Heads Off, as he learned the ways of his
wife's people. It had never been so in his homeland.

Farther from the fire were the younger warriors, still in
concentric circles. Those of unproven status or those
with less interest in the Council scattered around the
perimeter. Entirely outside the Council circle, children
wandered idly, or ran in play among the lodges. Occasionally it was necessary for some adult to rise and ad-
monish the youngsters to silence in respect for the Big
Council.

The chiefs would arrive last, but lesser warriors were
gathering. As the circle began to fill, it became apparent
to Coyote that the ranks were thin behind the seat of the
chief of the Elk-dog band. He glanced over the crowd
with alarm, and quickly recognized that those not in
evidence were the followers of young Badger.

Coyote's concern mounted. What could the Bloods be
planning? He idled away from the council site, then
turned and hurried to the lodge of Heads Off. Tall One
was just finishing the braiding of her husband's hair.

"Come in, Father," she called, glancing up from her
task. "We are almost ready."

She took down the shiny Spanish bit from its place,
and reverently placed its thong around her husband's
neck. Originally, the glittering object had been used in
the mouth of the young chief's gray mare, the first elk-
dog the People had ever seen. Now it was recognized as a
most powerful talisman, the elk-dog medicine of Heads
Off. It was used only as a symbolic amulet, worn around
the neck of the young chief, and then only for special
occasions. Coyote remained silent, gazing at the little
reflections of firelight from the dangling silver ornaments.
Though he himself had had a major part in the events
surrounding this strongest of medicines, he was still in
awe. The elk-dog medicine was far more powerful even
than he had at first realized. Its profound effect on the
entire tribe had caused great change in the People's way
of living. Greater, perhaps, than any other medicine since
First Man and First Woman crawled from the earth through
the hollow log.

Coyote returned from his reverie, aware that his son-in-law had spoken to him.

"I said, Uncle," Heads Off was asking, "is the Council nearly ready to begin?"

It was important, Tall One had taught her husband, for him to arrive at the proper time. Not too early, before chiefs of the other bands, but at about the same time. And above all, he should arrive before the Real-chief. To come later would not show proper respect.

The predicament was solved simply, by finishing his preparations, and then waiting near the lodge until the chiefs of the other bands were seen approaching the fire.

Coyote held the skin door-flap aside and Heads Off stepped through, pausing outside to let his eyes adjust to the darkness. Tall One stood beside him, holding his arm proudly.

Coyote cleared his throat uneasily. "Something is wrong," he said softly. "The Bloods have not come to the Council."

"Where are they?" The young chief was instantly alert. His wife's hand at his elbow tightened, almost imperceptibly.

"I do not know, Heads Off. It is only that their places are empty."

Tall One spoke, anxiously. "Surely they would not dishonor the Elk-dog band by staying away from the Big Council!"

Long Elk stepped from the shadows and motioned impatiently. It was time to make their appearance. Uneasily, the little group moved forward, pausing to allow the medicine man to join them. Heads Off spoke to him.

The Bloods have not come to the Council, Uncle."

"*Aiee*, they will come to no good." White Buffalo threw up his hands in despair.

They could see old Black Beaver of the Mountain band picking his way among his seated warriors. Heads Off quickened his step, and reached his place just as White Bear of the Red Rocks entered the circle of firelight. The chiefs exchanged nods of greeting, and Heads Off sat on the robe spread out for him. On either side and slightly to the rear were Coyote and White Buffalo. Tall One sat unobtrusively behind him, close enough to make her presence comforting. It had been painfully obvious that the ranks of warriors of the Elk-dog band were thin.

Heads Off watched the patter of conversation around the circle. He was certain everyone was talking about the Elk-dogs, and the absence of their warriors. Damn those young idiots, he brooded. How could they shame their band and their families? The entire tribe would see their lack of respect for their chief and his council.

Heads Off sat, furious, attempting to appear calm and unruffled. A murmur arose behind him, and people began to crane their necks to look. Finally he too turned to see the cause of the commotion.

The Bloods were arriving. In the lead stepped Badger, tall and proud, and fully armed. He wore his ceremonial headdress as if for a warriors' dance rather than a council. Behind him walked his followers. All were dressed like their leader, for a warriors' dance, and across each of their foreheads was painted the broad crimson stripe.

The young men made no special moves, but merely paraded pompously through the astonished crowd and seated themselves.

And none too soon. From among the lodges to the north side of the circle stepped proud old Many Robes with his sub-chiefs. Heads Off breathed a sigh of relief. At least the Bloods had not made the unforgivable error of arriving after the Real-chief.

Many Robes strode into the circle and seated himself, motioning to his pipe bearer. The ornate ceremonial pipe of the People emerged from its case, was filled, and handed to the Real-chief. The pipe bearer brought a brand from the fire, and the old chief ceremonially lighted the leafy mixture in the bowl. Many Robes concealed well his doubts. *Aiee*, watching them from the darkness, he had begun to wonder if those young hotheads would ever show up. Fortunately, he had been able to postpone his entrance to allow the Elk-dog band to save face.

There still remained grave doubts as to what was afoot. Why were the young men dressed for a ceremonial dance, and with their cursed red paint on their faces?

Outwardly, the Real-chief was calm as he methodically puffed smoke to the four winds, to the earth and sky, and handed the pipe to Black Beaver. That chief repeated the ritual, and the pipe moved on around the circle. Many Robes, receiving it back after each had performed the ceremony, knocked the dottle from the bowl and handed it to his pipe bearer. He cleared his throat to open the Big Council.

"Hear me, my chiefs! The People have gathered for the Sun Dance. Let each chief speak for his band."

Black Beaver rose slowly and addressed the Council.

"I am Black Beaver, chief of the Mountain band of the People. We have wintered well, and the hunting was good. We have seen no enemy."

The Mountain chief's message was always brief and to the point, observed Heads Off. White Bear rose, made the customary speech, and noted that they had seen a traveling band of Head Splitters.

"Their families were with them, as we had ours," he continued, "so we had no fighting."

This attracted very little attention. Such meetings were commonplace. Next came the Elk-dog band. Heads Off stood.

"I am Heads Off, of the Elk-dog band," he began. "We wintered well, but game was scarce this greening time." There was a mutter of discontent behind him. Perhaps, he thought, our plan was more obvious than we thought.

"Some of our warriors have had skirmishes with the Head Splitters. We lost one young man."

He sat down again. Be damned, he thought at the rising mutter behind him, if I give you the satisfaction of telling about your kills. The commotion continued, and people began to turn to look. Heads Off turned also. Badger was rising to his feet.

"My chief!" he practically shouted. "That is not all! We have struck the enemy. We have . . ."

"Silence!" Few people present had ever heard Many Robes raise his voice in Council before. "Take your seat! When you are a chief you may speak in Council. Until that time you will be silent!"

The stern visage and flinty stare of the Real-chief was not to be denied. By sheer force of will he took control of the situation as Badger faltered, became confused, and humbly sank to his seat.

Heads Off was embarrassed for the young man, but exhilarated by the manner in which the Real-chief had handled the matter. His respect for old Many Robes continued to increase.

The expression on the face of the Real-chief was now reverting to normal, stern but tolerant and benign. He turned expectantly to the Eastern band. Their chief rose quickly.

"Yes, my chief. I am Small Ears of the Eastern Band."

Small Ears' message continued, but the rest of the Council was anticlimax. The Bloods sat quietly, chastised by the strength of the Real-chief. The Council adjourned, and the People began to scatter to their lodges for the night.

10

» » »

The Bloods were disgruntled at their treatment in the Big Council. The People continued to ignore them, and the young dissidents reacted by being more active, loud, and obnoxious.

Badger presented himself at the Sun Dance lodge on the first day of the dance, in his symbolic red paint, accompanied by his followers. For a moment it appeared that the keeper of the Sun Dance would prevent their entering. Still, one's participation in the Sun Dance was a very private and personal thing. Each performed according to the dictates of his own conscience. There were some who even danced backward, or wore some strange article of decoration, perhaps to fulfill a secret vow.

In the end, the sentry decided that there was nothing so unusual in the Bloods' facial paint. They were allowed to enter and participate in the dance.

It seemed, however, as the days passed, that Badger became more irritable. Apparently, his militant challenge to tribal authority could stand almost anything but the good-natured tolerance of the tribe. This had always been the way of the People. If one does no harm to the group, let him do as he wishes.

So, through the entire Sun Dance, the Bloods seemed angry and frustrated that they could get no reaction of any sort from the People. They paraded pompously around the camp, noisy and insolent, attempting to create an incident, but were completely ignored.

Perhaps this was why, on the morning after the last all-night session of the dance, Badger was looking for trouble. Irritably, he presented himself at White Buffalo's lodge.

"Uncle!" he called out. There was no trace of respect in his voice. "We wish a vision for the hunt."

The old man was tired. The rigors of the Sun Dance were a trying time, even for younger men. Sleepily, he rolled out of his robes, but not before Badger was calling out again and slapping the skin cover of the lodge. The medicine man held the doorflap aside and Badger stooped to enter.

"We would hunt buffalo," he demanded. "Give us a vision!"

It was a command rather than a request.

"My son, the tribe will be moving. Today is no time to start a hunt."

Badger's eyes burned into the old man's face, cruel and relentless. For the first time in many years, White Buffalo was physically afraid. And of one of his own band, he thought sadly.

Reluctantly, he turned and prepared to perform the dance. Crow Woman readied the drum and the medicine man donned his buffalo robe. Not the sacred white cape, but an ordinary robe was used for this ceremony. The muffled rhythm of the drum set the cadence, and the medicine man began his shuffling, stamping dance. He pawed the ground like a massive herd bull, and swung his head and shoulders in imitation of the great beasts.

White Buffalo was just warming to the challenge of the dance when his visitor rudely interrupted.

"Enough, old man!" Badger injected. "Throw the stones!"

Crow Woman, astonished at the effrontery of the youth, stopped the drumbeat and sat, openmouthed. No one had ever dared interrupt a ceremonial dance. The medicine man straightened slowly and stared hard at Badger.

"No good will come of this."

"Throw the stones!" It was now a command, and the old man moved to comply, not quite understanding why he did so.

The medicine man turned and unrolled a bundled skin to spread before them. Its smooth painted surface bore geometric designs which shone dully in the dim light of the lodge. He produced a pouch, heavily embroidered with quillwork, and shook the contents into his gnarled palm.

With a dramatic gesture, he rolled the handful of small objects onto the surface of the spread skin. They scattered and bounced, settling to rest as he squatted to interpret the cast. Painted plum stones, small bits of bone, wood, and brightly colored pebbles settled in a pattern on the skin. White Buffalo studied the objects, muttering to himself, and occasionally poked at a stone with a knobby forefinger. Finally he looked up, directly at the waiting Badger.

"My son, it is not good. I do not fully understand the cast, but danger and death are here!"

"You lie, old man! Throw again!"

White Buffalo shook his head.

"I can make but one cast. Then the medicine is gone." An idea suddenly occurred to him. "But, I can cast the black stones."

Seldom used, the black stones were reserved for special purposes. Five in number, they had been handed down through successions of medicine men of the People. No one, except the medicine man himself, had ever been allowed to examine the black stones closely, and for very good reason.

The black stones were completely predictable in their forecast. Five plum stones had been painted black on one side, in a manner similar to the ordinary half-red gambling stones in common use. Their difference, aside from color, was subtle. The plum stones had been selected long ago, and painted by a skilled medicine man in the distant past. White Buffalo had once examined them closely, and determined their secret.

The selected plum stones were slightly flattened on one side, a freak of growth not obvious to casual observation in the dim light of a medicine man's lodge. The observer would be intent on looking for color, not shape. Would there be more stones showing the black-painted, or the natural yellow side when the cast was made? The medicine man already knew that the black sides would predominate. He could use the black stones to enforce any advice or vision he might wish. They were seldom used, and then very cautiously, but White Buffalo felt that this was the time.

The clutter of objects on the medicine skin was gathered and returned to the pouch. Crow Woman ceremonially smoothed the skin for the coming ritual. White Buffalo turned, rummaged in his equipment, and produced a tiny pouch lavishly decorated with quills and paint. He handled it reverently, carefully. He must be cautious, for Badger was clever and observant.

With slow and symbolic motions, he opened the sack and shook out the five small plum stones. He drew forth their cup, made from the tip of a buffalo horn, and placed the stones carefully in it. The polished horn gleamed black as he held it aloft and chanted the ritual phrases. Then, with a dramatic gesture, he swept his arm downward and over the skin, tumbling the stones across its surface.

Badger watched, fascinated, as the black stones skittered and bounced, finally coming to rest. Four of the five showed the black surface, the other the natural yellow color.

"*Aiee*, it is bad, as I have said," intoned the pleased medicine man.

"It is a trick!" Badger almost shouted. He reached quickly forward and scooped the scattered stones in his hand.

White Buffalo, taken completely by surprise, could only sit numbly at the unexpected turn of events. The young man was shaking the black stones between his palms. How had he solved the secret so quickly?

Badger cast the stones back onto the skin, and watched, fascinated, as they skittered, rolled, and came to rest. He stared at the result. This time all five showed the black surface. Anger began to mount in the young man's face. In that moment, White Buffalo realized the truth. Badger had not solved the secret. He was only angry that the medicine of the stones had gone against him.

With a swing of his arm, the insolent young man swept the stones from the medicine skin. They bounced and jumped around the lodge, one falling almost into the fire. In the moment of silence, one stone struck the tightly drawn skin of the lodge cover beside Crow Woman with a soft thunk. She absently picked it up and stared at it.

"It is a trick of some sort! We go anyway!" Badger jumped to his feet and strode from the lodge.

11

>> >> >>

Crow Woman and White Buffalo looked at each other in stunned silence for a few heartbeats. Then the old woman began to move around, clucking her tongue disapprovingly as she retrieved the black plum stones. The last one was elusive, but she finally found it, in the ashes near the fire.

White Buffalo examined the objects briefly, and returned them to their pouch with the horn cup. He was disturbed. Obviously, the Blood Society intended to go on their hunt, regardless of the medicine man's approval. It was a very awkward situation. The Elk-dog band should be preparing for departure. Instead, they must either wait for the Bloods to return, or, if need be, leave without them. Neither course was a good one. Once again, the youngsters had caused embarrassment to their band and their families.

White Buffalo hurried over to the chief's lodge, intending to inform him of the developments. He found Heads Off standing outside, watching the activity. Badger was riding among the lodges, calling to his followers and announcing the hunt.

"I gave them bad omens, Heads Off. They go anyway."

Coyote joined them and the three watched the rising excitement of the young men as the group of mounted hunters grew.

Coyote spoke. "We will leave tomorrow even if they have not returned?"

Heads Off did not answer. He was still pondering that question in his own mind. Also, the old apprehension was growing as he watched the Bloods wheeling their horses and shouting to each other. This did not look like the start of a hunting trip. They should be calm and businesslike. Instead, they were working each other into a frenzy of excitement. There appeared to be no doubt about it. This was no hunting trip. This was a war party!

Their numbers grew as they organized, and even from a distance the three could see that the Bloods were being joined by young men from other bands. *Aiee*, it appeared that there were now more mounted warriors than one has fingers and toes.

A man on foot strode among the lodges and approached the horsemen. Heads Off recognized Sees Far, and in a moment saw the object of that warrior's attention. The man angrily approached a rider that they now recognized as his errant son, and an argument ensued.

It was too far away to hear the words of the argument, but the situation was plain. Sees Far was forbidding his son to go with the Bloods, and the boy was insisting on his right to do so. The argument was still at an impasse when Badger arrogantly rode up and entered the conversation. Sees Far turned angrily to the young man, and voices rose in argument.

Heads Off realized the danger and sprinted forward. The adversaries were well over a hundred paces away, and before he had covered half the distance, the inevitable had happened. Sees Far, with a shout of anger, rushed at Badger's horse. The animal shied away, and the young man swung a weapon, which fortunately missed its target. Sees Far snatched at the reins, and pulled the animal's head around as Badger struck at him a second time.

The older warrior dodged the blow, but grasped the wrist of his assailant, shaking the club loose from his grip. Sees Far was not a big man, but seemed suddenly to acquire superior strength as he gave a mighty heave and pulled Badger bodily from his horse. The young man landed heavily, but sprang up immediately and grappled with Sees Far, the two falling again to the ground. Struggling and kicking, the pair rolled almost under the trampling feet of the frightened horse.

Heads Off, nearly winded from his run, was approaching as a cluster of people crowded forward to see the struggle. The rolling pair was obscured from his view for a moment, and he elbowed forward, pushing the horse aside.

Badger was just rising, breathing heavily.

"He would have killed me!" The voice was almost pleading.

Heads Off looked at the still figure, face down in the dust. He knelt, and gently rolled Sees Far toward him. A trickle of blood from a gash in the upper belly puddled in the dust. The far-seeing eyes which had earned this warrior the respect of the tribe now gazed sightlessly at the sun.

An angry mutter arose from the gathering crowd. Badger looked from one face to another, desperately seeking support, but meeting only enmity.

"I had no choice! He attacked me!"

"Sees Far was not armed," a woman stated quietly, and the angry mutter spread.

Coyote came puffing to the scene, squatting beside Heads Off to talk rapidly.

"Heads Off, it is a matter for the Big Council. I have sent for the Real-chief."

The People were still numb with the shock of the thing. It was the worst of all taboos, that one of the People should kill another. Though violence and death were commonplace, there was this most absolute of laws. One does not kill a member of the tribe.

Badger was still looking helplessly around the circle for nonexistent encouragement when the Real-chief arrived, flanked by two sub-chiefs of the Northern band. The crowd separated to allow them to approach. The keen old eyes of Many Robes took in the situation at a glance. The wife of Sees Far was now at his side, sobbing quietly. Her son, the cause of the episode, stood staring in shocked silence.

"You, boy," the Real-chief addressed him crisply. "You

have much to answer for. You must be a great help to
your mother now."

Many Robes turned to the hapless Badger. That young
man started to speak, then thought better of it and stood
silent under the scathing gaze of the Real-chief.

"You will go to your lodge and stay there until the Big
Council meets at dark. The men will come for you."

He turned and spoke more quietly to Heads Off.

"Your warriors will bring him to the Council?"

Heads Off nodded. He was heartsick that his, the Elk-
dog band, should be the origin of such disgrace among
his adopted people.

The Real-chief turned and the crowd parted again for
him. They began to disperse, animated conversations
beginning in small groups.

"Heads Off, there is much to do." It was Coyote, at his
elbow, bringing him back to reality.

White Buffalo had arrived, and now attempted to explain the necessary steps. The keening wail of the Mourning Song rose from the family of Sees Far as the medicine
man rapidly explained to his young chief.

"It is very bad medicine, Heads Off, for this to happen
at the Sun Dance. It may destroy all the good medicine
for the season. We must quickly remove the dead man,
so the evil deed will not taint the Sun Dance place."

Heads Off nodded. The body would be ceremonially
buried on an elevated scaffold in the trees, but in an area
removed from the Sun Dance lodge.

After the remains were wrapped in robes and carried
downstream nearly half a sun's journey, the spot where
the tragedy had taken place was ceremonially cleansed
by White Buffalo. Most of the Elk-dog band accompanied
the family to the site of the burial scaffold. Sees Far had
been a respected warrior.

By the time the band had carried out the required
rituals and returned to the Sun Dance site, it was growing late. Sun Boy and his torch were slipping below
earth's rim. It was time for the convening of the Big
Council.

12
>> >> >>

"**W**hat will be done?" Heads Off asked his father-in-law as they approached the Big Council. Every man, woman and child in the entire tribe was present. None wished to miss the important decisions brought on by this tragic event.

"I do not know, Heads Off. Such a thing has not happened in my lifetime."

"There was once such a matter before I was born," spoke White Buffalo from the other side, "but I do not remember what was done to the killer."

In his own homeland, the penalty would be prison or death, reflected Heads Off. But he realized the complete difference of this situation. It had never occurred to him to wonder how the People meted out punishment to breakers of the tribal law.

"He will probably be banished," observed White Buffalo.

They reached the circle and seated themselves, and none too soon. The Real-chief and his cortege were approaching.

By contrast with the relaxed slow-moving formality of previous sessions of the Big Council, this gathering progressed rapidly. Many Robes hurried through the ritual smoke and ordered the offender brought to the Council.

Badger was allowed to speak, and made again the point that he had acted only in self-defense when attacked.

The woman who had been nearest to the brief fight again stated that Sees Far had been unarmed.

Another man, one of the older warriors, asked and received permission to speak.

"My chiefs," he glanced around the circle, "none of this has any meaning. The important thing is only that one of our warriors has killed a man of his own, the People." He sat down without waiting to see the reaction.

Several others spoke, all to the same effect. The law was absolute on this point. There was simply no worse crime among the People. Badger began to look more and more desperate. Heads Off could almost feel sorry for the young man.

"It is enough!" Many Robes finally ended the discussion. "The Council will vote. Shall Badger, who has killed one of our own, be banished?"

To be banished was virtually a death sentence. A person expelled would be forbidden, on pain of death, to enter the camp of any band of his former tribe. He would be a person adrift, with no home, friends, or relatives. It might be possible, Coyote had told his son-in-law earlier, that if Badger were banished he could live among the Grower tribes along the river. Another possibility would be to approach the Head Splitters and throw himself on their mercy. Heads Off thought it unlikely that a proud young man like Badger would take either action. He would prefer to take his chances alone on the prairie. His young wife, Heads Off had learned, would have the option of following her disgraced husband or returning to her parents' lodge.

Many Robes now called for the vote.

"The Mountain band?" he inquired expectantly.

Old Black Beaver silently nodded, voting the affirmation for expulsion.

"Red Rocks?"

Chief White Bear, too, gave the silent nod.

"Elk-dog band?"

"My chief, I withhold the vote."

Heads Off had struggled with the decision. He now

realized that it was too emotionally loaded a situation for him to decide in a rational manner. The Real-chief nodded acknowledgment of the abstention, and moved on around the circle.

"Eastern band?"

Small Ears solemnly inclined his head, and for practical purposes the vote was over. Many Robes spoke for the Northern band as well as in his capacity as Real-chief. He addressed Badger.

"You are no longer of the People. You have, by your act, shown this. Any of the People may turn you away, or kill you if they choose. By the time Sun Boy is overhead, you must be gone!"

Badger stood, surrounded by the People, no longer his people. He appeared about to speak, then changed his mind and shuffled away from the fire. His young wife rose, and tears streaming, followed him away. The crowd parted before them.

Then an amazing thing happened. As the couple reached the outer fringe of the circle, a young man leaped to his feet and faced the chiefs of the Council.

"I go with Badger!"

"I, too!" Another stood.

Within a few heartbeats, several young warriors were standing and shouting. Badger stopped, apparently surprised, and turned to look at the circle. His slumping shoulders drew up and back and he again assumed a stance of confidence and assurance. He seemed about to speak again. Many Robes had no intention of causing a further split in the tribe by allowing Badger a speech.

"The Council is ended," he announced, rising to depart.

The crowd split into a score of smaller groups, buzzing with excitement. Badger and his followers drew aside, becoming noisier and more confident as they attracted more young men.

Heads Off felt as though a great weight had lifted from his shoulders. All the doubts and indecision of the past few moons had in a few hours been resolved. Even under the tragic circumstances, even with the tearing apart of families and mourning of mothers for departing sons, at least something decisive had happened. He watched as the Bloods began excited preparations for their departure at daylight. They were making a festival of it.

"Go ask Red Dog," someone shouted. A rider loped away. There were more shouts, and excited laughter. Things were rapidly getting out of hand.

Heads Off felt a heavy, sick feeling in the pit of his stomach. It appeared that what should have been a disgrace for Badger, the instigator of the rebellion, was turning into a triumph. The young men did not realize the gravity of their decision.

"At least," Heads Off muttered to Coyote at his elbow, "it is over."

Coyote took a deep breath before he answered.

"No, my friend. It is only beginning!"

13
›› ›› ››

Sun Boy had hardly climbed above earth's rim to begin
his daily run when the first of the lodges came down. Of
the young warriors who considered themselves part of
the Blood Society, perhaps half had their own lodges. Of
these, nearly every wife had elected to follow her husband into exile. In addition, there were two couples on
the verge of marriage who also chose the way of the
outcast Bloods.

There was one girl, a warrior sister, who would accompany the Blood Society. She would live in her brother's
lodge. Her father, now well past his prime, simply threw
up his hands in helpless resignation.

A scattered handful of discontents from the other bands
joined them. The young single warriors among the Bloods
would live as guests in the lodges of their fellow warriors
until they established their own. In effect, the Bloods
were becoming a sixth band of the People. Except, Heads
Off thought with regret, they would never be of the
People. They would remain outcasts forever, a tiny tribe
of their own, with allegiance to no one. Their chances of
survival were slim to none. There would be none to help

or support them against the certain onslaught of the
Head Splitters. They could field not many more than a
score of warriors, certainly not enough for defense.

This seemed to make little difference to the defiant
Bloods. They systematically assisted each other with preparations for travel, and soon Badger, astride his big black
stallion, led them through the camp and out onto the
prairie. It would have been easier and more logical, Heads
Off noticed, to enter the prairie directly and circle the
campsite. Badger chose instead to use his departure for
one last irritating gesture. Dust, kicked up by the horses,
drifted among the lodges and over the cooking areas.
Angry women called threats after the horsemen.

The final insult was that a handful of young Bloods,
bringing up the rear, drove the loose animals of the group
through the camp, causing even more havoc.

A young man reined over to stop before his chief for a
moment. Heads Off recognized Red Dog. He had been a
promising student in the Rabbit Society, and had become
an expert horseman. The band would sorely miss such a
warrior.

"I am sorry, Heads Off. You have been good to me. I
have learned much from you!"

The young chief sensed some indecision here, and
started to speak, but then changed his mind. What use
would it be? He smiled and nodded, feeling a bit foolish.

Red Dog whirled his mare and trotted after the departing Bloods.

Dust began to settle as the little band filed out onto
the prairie. Here and there a wail of grief told of a bereaved parent. Heads Off had seen tears in the eyes of
several of the departing Bloods' young wives, too. It was
a sad parting. It was unlikely that any of the young
people filing over the hill would ever be seen again. He
turned to find Coyote standing beside him.

"It is an evil day," the other said simply.

The two turned to look at the campsite of the Elk-dog
band. Here and there were scarred circles where the lodges
of the defectors had stood. The remaining lodges looked
pitifully few. With a sudden start, Heads Off realized the
reason for the depressed attitude of Coyote.

The Elk-dog band had become smaller by some ten
lodges, and perhaps twice as many warriors. He had been

concerned about the inability of the Bloods to defend themselves. Now the gravity of the situation sank home to him for the first time. Would his own Elk-dog band be able to mount a defense? Their fighting strength had just been reduced by over one third.

Apparently this fact had not been overlooked by the other bands. Small Ears stopped by and generously offered to allow the Elk-dogs to join his Eastern band. Heads Off politely refused. He had had enough problems, he reflected, because of people with poor judgment. He did not need the added stigma of association with the Eastern band, traditionally a foolish group.

More welcome was the invitation by the Red Rocks to camp together for a season. These two had spent a winter in the same camp before, in fact, the year his son Eagle was born.

The suggestion of the Red Rocks was taken more seriously, then, but at length rejected.

Heads Off talked long with both Coyote and White Buffalo before making the decision. Coyote was initially in favor of joining the other band. The old run-and-hide philosophy, held by the People before the coming of the elk-dog, was still strong.

Oddly, the old medicine man favored striking out boldly on their own. The lifting of his burden by the banishment of the Bloods had taken years from his age. He now appeared vigorous, even eager. The Red Rocks, he pointed out, winter in an area with little game. It would be difficult to obtain food for the combined bands.

In additon, there was the matter of prestige. The Elk-dogs, most respected of the bands of the People, could not appear to be merely the poor relatives of another group.

"Perhaps next year," White Buffalo conceded, "but not now."

In the end, Coyote agreed. For this season, they would be on their own.

Heads Off was uneasy about it, but concurred. He was thinking of his family. Their son Eagle was at a vulnerable age. Tall One would soon give birth again. Finally he conceded that the threat of short food supply with the Red Rocks was a greater threat than that of a chance encounter with Head Splitters. Word was spread that the Elk-dogs would move on the following day.

He would lead the band southeast into the southern end of the Tall Grass Hills. The rolling, broken country there would allow for more defensible positions.

When the Elk-dog band filed over the hill next morning, he was shocked to see how pitifully small the group looked. A quick count revealed that they were missing more lodges than expected.

"*Aiee*, they scatter in the wind," commented Coyote philosophically.

Again, Heads Off suffered shock and now the pain of rejection. The People could change loyalties and join another band very simply. It required merely to follow whichever group they chose after the Sun Dance.

There were some who switched loyalties readily, spending each season with the band which appeared to have the greatest prestige. The Elk-dog band had grown in this manner each season since Heads Off had been among them.

But now, in addition to the Bloods, three more lodges had switched allegiance, and the Elk-dogs' strength was dangerously reduced again. Heads Off experienced a momentary surge of anger at the desertion.

Then he began to think more calmly. Warriors with such inconstant allegiance would hardly be worth their presence in battle anyway, he told himself glumly. He was probably better off without such undependable followers.

He felt somewhat better after this period of rationalization, but deep in his heart, he did not believe it at all.

14
>> >> >>

Heads Off called a council at the end of the first day's travel. It could be seen by all that the band was seriously under fighting strength, and it was necessary to recognize the fact and plan for it.

There was one encouraging note as the Elk-dogs made camp that evening. One more family, traveling late, joined them just before dark. Heads Off recognized one of the young warriors of the Red Rocks band, who had helped on a foray against the Head Splitters. How long ago, it now seemed. The People had set out to obtain horses, and Heads Off, still an outsider, had helped to organize the raid.

"May we join you? We wish to see new country."

The chief nodded in welcome, and the newcomers hastened to establish camp before dark.

Heads Off was grateful. It was obvious that this young warrior understood the plight of the Elk-dog band. Every warrior they could muster might be needed in the coming moons. Even one spear, one bowman, might make the critical difference to survival.

This, of course, was to be the theme of the evening's

council. Appearance would be all-important as they traveled. It must not be easy for any casual observer to see that the band was reduced in number.

With this in mind, Heads Off outlined the basic plan he and Coyote had discussed during travel. They must appear to have as many lodges as possible. Each family unit would loan a lodge pole or two. The extra poles would be tied in bundles of ten or twelve, and dragged by a spare horse.

Thus, an observer from a distant hilltop might count the number of horses drawing lodge poles. There would appear to be several more lodges, perhaps four more, than actually existed. Allowing two warriors per lodge, that would cause an enemy to overestimate the strength of the band by eight or more warriors.

Additionally, as the council discussed the matter, another idea or two emerged. An old warrior of the Bowstring Society spoke.

"If we spread out instead of follow single file as we travel, it will leave a bigger trail."

There were nods and murmurs of agreement. A broad multiple track made by many poles would imply many lodges, to anyone coming upon the trail.

A woman suggested that the usual manner of packing might be altered. Each family could distribute the customary assortment of baggage among as many animals as possible. Again, an observer would see many laden packhorses, and assume a strong, affluent, and presumably, well-armed band.

People began to be drawn into the enthusiasm of the thing, and suggestions rippled around the circle. Someone pointed out that the youngsters of the Rabbit Society should ride and carry weapons wherever possible. From a little distance, the age and maturity of an armed rider would be difficult to evaluate.

Tall One addressed her husband.

"My chief, could not the younger women dress in their husbands' garments and carry weapons?"

"No one would take you for a warrior, mother!" The speaker was Coyote, poking fun at his daughter's very pregnant abdomen. The circle rocked with laughter.

"It is good!" Heads Off was pleased with the idea.

Perhaps not those with small children, but many could pass as warriors.

The young women whispered together excitedly. Heads Off felt that this was good strategy. Not only would it give the appearance of more warriors, but some of the girls were quite adept with weapons.

He had thought it strange, when he first joined the People, that both girls and boys took instruction in the Rabbit Society. His own wife, the Tall One, had been able to outrun him before her pregnancy with Eagle. She was skilled with the bow, a weapon he had never considered his best. And many of the older women, he knew, were expert with the throwing stick. He had seen Big Footed Woman, his mother-in-law, knock a rabbit cleanly with the short, heavy instrument. The women of the People had the knowledge and skills, and in an emergency attack, every weapon might be needed.

The council broke up on an optimistic note. People scattered to their sleeping robes.

"Do you think there will be trouble, my husband?" Tall One always called him "my husband," especially in an emotional situation. She snuggled against him, the firm bulge of her abdomen reminding him of their vulnerability in case of attack.

"Do *you* think so?" he evasively returned the question. "You know the People better than I."

"I do not know. If the Head Splitters think we are weak, they will try to kill us."

Yes, he thought, drawing her close, or steal our women. He remembered that, when he had first seen the traditional enemy, he had been told, ". . . they steal our women. Our women are much prettier than theirs."

Now, that threat was much closer to his own awareness. He pulled Tall One protectively to the shelter of his arms and held her gently.

"Then," he stated positively, "we must be ready."

He wished he really felt as confident as he tried to sound.

15
》 》 》

Whuen the Elk-dog band resumed travel next morning, there was an entirely different mood. The depression of the previous day had been replaced by good-natured optimism. Young women, who had rebraided their hair in masculine style, donned garments of their husbands or fathers. They strutted around, brandishing weapons and looking completely like lithe young warriors, while families and friends joked and made fun.

A number of women with young children pooled the youngsters under the care of one or two mothers, while the others took part in the deception. Heads Off was glad to see that the women handled the weapons well. There was some practicing in evidence, and a good-natured wager or two on a trial shot with the bow. Their proficiency was quite acceptable. The chief devoutly hoped that the ability of these young women in combat would never be tested. But it was well to be prepared.

It was not entirely unheard of, among the People, for a woman to take up arms. There were stories of women who had stood fast in defense of their husbands in time of attack. One old woman was called "Bear's Rump

Woman." As a young bride, the story said, she had once thrust a spear into the posterior of a bear that was mauling her husband. The startled animal had fled, squealing, and she had proudly worn the name ever since.

So, although the People might joke about armed women, and exaggerate the situation in pretense, the basic approach was deadly serious. A capable woman was highly respected, and a source of pride for her husband.

The spirit of playacting extended to the teenagers. Several young men solemnly pretended to be heads of their own lodges. They tied the borrowed lodge poles to elk-dogs belonging to their parents, and prepared to join the procession as the band moved out.

Heads Off mounted his gray mare and cantered to a nearby hilltop to get the general effect. He was amazed at the change in appearance of the Elk-dog band. Had he not known of the subterfuge he would have thought their fighting strength doubled since the previous day. He rejoined the column, pleased and more confident. He doubted that a stranger to the group would notice that there were very few loose horses. Nearly every available animal carried a burden.

The band traveled well, raising a commendably spectacular plume of dust. Certainly a chance observer would be impressed with the size and strength of such a unit.

It was three suns before they encountered anyone. The advance scouts hurried back to tell of an approaching column. The strangers appeared to be a traveling band of Head Splitters.

The People drew together, became more alert, and continued in the same general direction. It would be another of the usual noncombative confrontations. Both groups would wish to avoid fighting, with families present, but sometimes, something could ignite the spark of combat. It could be a touchy moment.

The front of the column reached a low ridge and Heads Off saw that the meeting would occur in a grassy flat ahead. He beckoned to Long Elk, Standing Bird, and Coyote, and the four rode forward to meet the advancing party from the other band.

"Stay well back, and bear around them to the left," he called over his shoulder.

To himself, he voiced the hope that none of his people

overplay the thing. If the enemy discovered the extent of
the subterfuge, it would become immediately apparent
that there must be a reason for it. Maybe, Heads Off told
himself grimly, this entire thing wasn't too good an idea.
It might only call attention to the fact that something
was wrong among the People.

Now they were approaching the other chief and his
cortege. Both groups reined in and stepped forward at a
walk, hands raised in greeting. The Head Splitter chief
looked familiar, one the People had seen before. Oppos-
ing chiefs often became acquainted in this way, by repeated encounters from year to year.

"*Ah-koh*, Hair Face," spoke the other, in word and
sign. "How is it with you?"

"It goes well," Heads Off replied with sign talk. "Bull's
Tail, I believe you are called?"

The other nodded, and ran his glance over the Elk-dog
band as they skirted the meadow at a little distance.
Heads Off held his breath and tried to appear casual.
Would the other chief see anything unusual in the column? His gaze followed the Head Splitter's, and he could
plainly see the telltale shape of a well-formed leg here
and there against a dark horse, and the outline of ample
bosoms in loose-fitting, male shirts.

Apparently the significance was lost on the enemy
chief.

"Your young men ride well," Bull's Tail observed.

"Yes, they are well taught," Heads Off answered quickly.
"You have found game?" It might be as well to change
the subject.

The other nodded. "We have seen many buffalo. Our
children are fat and our women happy. And you?"

"All we can use," Heads Off nodded, "but just now, we
come from our Big Council."

It would do no harm to reveal this fact. Their back
trail was plain anyway, if anyone wanted to follow it. To
tell the precise truth about that event would lend cre-
dence to the rest of the conversation.

"You met to the west of here? How far? Two, three
suns?"

This was logical conversation. The other band would
not wish to travel into country recently hunted out by a
large meeting of the People.

"No, four," Heads Off indicated. "Nearly straight west."

Bull's Tail nodded again. "Then we will go farther south," he announced, picking up his reins.

The two chiefs cautiously backed their horses a few steps, then turned and rode slowly back toward their respective groups.

"Do you think he tells truth about where they go?" asked Long Elk.

Coyote shrugged. "Who knows? That is what he wishes us to believe."

Heads Off glanced over his shoulder at the retreating party from the Head Splitter band. Bull's Tail was staring intently after the now distant Elk-dog column. Did he suspect something? The young chief wasn't sure. In fact, even much later, after the events of later moons, Heads Off was never certain in his own mind whether the Head Splitter had fathomed their secret.

16
>> >> >>

The area for summer camp was chosen carefully with defensibility in mind. A large number of people with many horses required a dependable water supply, as well as grass for the elk-dogs. A level grassy flat which spread within a long loop of the river served both purposes. As well, the river formed a difficult approach from three sides. Only from the north could a mass attack by mounted warriors come.

Behind the village area, to the west, the river crowded through a rocky ravine, shaded by massive oaks and cottonwoods. The broken nature of the rock-strewn gully, and the heavy growth of brush and timber, would furnish a thousand hiding places. Heads Off remembered grimly how, a few seasons previously he had ridiculed the "run-and-hide" philosophy of the People. Now he found himself assisting in planning for the same eventuality.

The young chief walked alone to the top of a low hill overlooking the village. The People were establishing a semipermanent camp, one to be used for several moons. He saw with amusement that some of the youngsters, still in the spirit of charade, were setting up make-believe lodges. A few poles, some old lodge skins, and the appearance was easily that of another lodge. To a distant observer, that would mean one or two more warriors. The total appearance of the camp was that of a strong and well-armed band.

Unless, he thought with some apprehension, unless the subterfuge is detected, then the whole thing could go wrong. Perhaps, Heads Off tried to reassure himself, no Head Splitters would be in the area this season. It was not unknown to go an entire season, even two, without an encounter.

Deep in his heart, he knew this was a false hope. The Head Splitters would have encountered the hot-headed young Bloods, who were looking for trouble. Then, having exterminated the reckless youngsters, they would realize something else: somewhere there was a band of the People whose young warriors were gone. They would be eager to attack the relatively defenseless band.

Perhaps they might even be aware that the vulnerable camp was that of Hair Face, the hated outsider. The Head Splitters would dearly love a chance for revenge after their defeat at the Great Battle. Perhaps, after all, the Elk-dogs should join the Red Rocks for a season or two.

Heads Off drew a deep sigh. It was ironic that his presence, originally the salvation of the People, had now become one of their biggest dangers. Why had he ever consented to the leadership of the band? He should have gotten as far away as possible, and as rapidly. In his mind's eye, he relived the events of some seasons earlier. He could have climbed on his gray mare and headed south until he encountered some of his own people. He knew there were scattered Spanish settlements all through the southern part of the area called Tejas.

A woman, heavy with child, came out of a lodge far below, leading a small boy by the hand. She headed toward the river, and Heads Off watched her long stride, graceful even in the last moons of her pregnancy. He recognized Tall One, and his reverie was abruptly returned to proper perspective. He could not have left the People, he knew. If he had the whole thing to do again, he would do the same.

His only regret was that he felt that he had bungled his

responsibility. His wife, son, and unborn child depended on him for protection. So, too, did the entire Elk-dog band. And Heads Off now had serious doubts as to his ability to provide that protection.

He watched the torch of Sun Boy slide below earth's edge, and by the time he had walked down the hill in the soft twilight the young chief had reached two conclusions. First, he would learn the run-and-hide philosophy if necessary. He would fight if necessary. In short, he would do whatever was required to ensure the safety of his family and his people. For, these were now, completely and totally, his own, by virtue of their common danger and their willingness to stake their lives on his leadership.

His second conclusion was more a determination. Heads Off had resolved that he would allow no one to know of his doubts. He would give no hint that he thought their situation precarious. Even Coyote, yes, even Tall One, who knew his every thought, must not know his insecurity.

He walked through the dusk, the camp now lighted by cooking fires. People smiled, waved, and he nodded solemnly in answer. Would they be so friendly, he wondered, if they knew his doubts and fears? This was why they must not. He could not allow the People to think that their leader had doubts about his own ability to lead.

Actually, Tall One was much closer than he would have believed to an understanding of his thoughts. She had seen him climb the hill, and started to follow him, but then changed her mind. Her father stopped by a little later.

"Where is Heads Off?" Coyote asked. "We need to put out sentries."

Tall One pointed to the solitary figure on the hill.

"Heads Off makes private medicine, Father. He will come down soon."

Coyote took a long look, and nodded. A person's private medicine must be respected. He turned away.

Tall One picked up a waterskin and took young Eagle by the hand. She would have meat ready when her husband returned.

She knew he was troubled. It had been in his eyes today. But now they were in summer camp. The stress of travel was behind them. She could show him the extra little attentions that a man needs to make him feel the greatest and strongest warrior on the plains.

She could make her husband forget his troubles and doubts. At least, she smiled to herself, it had always been so.

17
>> >> >>

It seemed for some time that the fears of Heads Off had been groundless. There was no sign of the enemy. Buffalo were plentiful, and the racks of drying meat were full. Rawhide bags of winter provisions began to bulge behind the lodge linings. Soon it would be time to move to better winter quarters.

Heads Off continued to defer the move. Tall One's time for birthing was at hand, and he wished that event to be completed before the strenuous journey began. The Moon of Thunder and the Red Moon gave way to the Moon of Ripening before there was any change in the routine of preparing for winter. When it came, the change was in completely unexpected form.

It was near dawn and Heads Off was curled comfortably against the warmth of his wife's body. He had just wakened to change his position and Tall One murmured softly in her sleep and cuddled closer. Suddenly there was the sound of running hoofbeats, a shout, and more horses running. He sprang up and leaped toward the door skin.

"Yip-yip-yip ..." came the long falsetto yell that was

the war cry of the dreaded Head Splitters. He stepped
back and seized his buffalo lance, darting back out into
the gray of the false dawn. A frightened horse thundered
past him, striking him a glancing blow with a shoulder.
Heads Off threw himself sideways and stumbled against
the lodge. He saw that the horse had no rider.

Quickly he stepped around the lodge to make sure his
gray mare Lolita was tied securely. She snorted, excited,
and rolled white-ringed eyes at him, but quieted to his
touch. While he stood a moment and sleepily tried to
decide whether to mount or remain on foot, more horses
stampeded past, urged on by the yells of mounted enemy warriors behind. He dodged around, trying to keep
from being trampled and at the same time find a target
for his lance. A nearby lodge shuddered and jerked as a
horse ran full against it. Other stampeding animals buf-
feted the structure as they forced past, and it slowly
toppled. A woman screamed, and a child cried out in
pain.

Then it was over. Thick dust choked his lungs and he
coughed heavily, peering into the dusk after the fleeing
horses. He had not seen even one of the enemy.

Through the camp people called out, trying to locate
family members. There were cries of pain. A lodge cover,
collapsed onto the coals of its cooking fire, began to
smoke heavily. People ran to drag it free and stamp out
the smoldering portion.

Heads Off satisfied himself of the safety of his family,
then swung to Lolita's back.

"Over here!" he shouted from an open area. "All who
have elk-dogs!"

A scattering of men began to converge in the growing
light. Most men, like Heads Off, kept one of their best
horses tied at the lodge. It had been the loose herd that
the enemy had stampeded and driven off.

"Who was with the elk-dogs?" he asked as Standing
Bird rode up.

"Small Bear. He is dead."

The chief had assumed so. He had no need to ask
further. He knew that, no matter how the manner of the
young man's death, the head would bear the Head Splitters' identifying mark of the war club, the skull crushed

by a blow. But, there was no help for Small Bear now. He turned to more urgent things.

"How many elk-dogs are here?"

A quick glance around the camp revealed that all had arrived. His heart sank. There were hardly more than twenty. The band, he knew, could not move camp without more horses. Especially since the remaining animals were buffalo runners, not packhorses. They must recover enough animals to transport the big lodge covers, or the Elk-dog band would be forced to spend the winter here, in a poor winter location. He gave the arm signal to move out.

To chase the enemy with a small force was not as foolhardy as it might have seemed. Seldom would an enemy war party number more than twenty. They had not sought a fight, but only to steal horses. A stronger party of Head Splitters would have made an attack, enabling them to count honors.

Therefore Heads Off was confident as they pushed forward. It was probably a small party of the enemy, a horse-stealing raid. The People, twenty of the best warriors, on the best horses, could easily catch and engage a fight with the fleeing Head Splitters, encumbered by loose animals, and recover at least part of the herd.

The trail was plain in the morning dew, and they passed an exhausted foal with its dam standing by, head down and flanks heaving. His guess had been correct, then. The raiding party would push ahead to escape, leaving slower animals behind. He touched a heel to the gray mare's ribs, and urged her into a canter again.

Occasionally they could catch a glimpse of their quarry, far ahead in the distance. Suddenly Long Elk reined in beside the chief.

"Heads Off, something is wrong! There are only two or three riders with the elk-dogs!"

Heads Off shaded his eyes and peered ahead, but could distinguish nothing in the blur of distance. He would take Long Elk's word for it. The young man's vision was among the best in the band, especially since the death of Sees Far. Long Elk could easily see the eighth star in the constellation of the Seven Hunters.

The Seven Hunters, Coyote had explained to his son-in-law, make a wide circle each night around the Real-star,

where their lodge is located. One with good eyes can see
that the next to the last hunter is accompanied by his
dog. On a clear night, Heads Off could dimly see the
Dog-star.

But now, with wind and dust making his eyes water,
there was only a moving blur in the distance.

"*Aiee*, look!" There was a cry behind him.

All the warriors turned to look in the direction someone was pointing. A dirty gray smudge on the horizon
marked the site of the camp. As they looked, the smudge
became broader, blacker, and a column of smoke rose in
the still morning air.

Mother of God, we've been duped, Heads off fumed as
he jerked the mare around and slammed heels into her
ribs. The other riders wheeled and followed. How could
he have been so stupid, to fall for such a ruse? His
instructor in tactics at the academy, half a world away,
would have had cadets walking parade all day for such a
blunder. To split one's forces against an enemy of unknown strength was unforgivable. *Aiee*, as stupid as the
owl who catches a skunk and does not know that it
stinks. He reverted to thinking like one of the People.

There was no doubt that the camp had been attacked.
The spreading smoke attested to that. But how bad was
it? His heart ached with thoughts of his vulnerable wife
and son. It was all he could do to restrain the impulse to
push the mare till she dropped. But then, he realized, he
would be on foot.

Carefully he paced the animals, walking while they
caught their wind, then pushing on.

Sun Boy was nearly straight up when they arrived back
at the burning village. A handful of enemy riders, who
had apparently been watching all along, rode over the
ridge and out of sight, signing obscene gestures before
they disappeared.

Fully half the lodges were in flames. Thick, greasy
smoke stank of burning leather and meat. Anxiously,
Heads Off reined among ruined lodges toward his own.
The lathered mare stepped skittishly around a body with
the head grotesquely distorted, and they looked around
the last lodge.

The lodge of Heads Off and Tall One was in complete
ruin, all their winter supplies greasy ashes. Almost fran-

tic, he leaped from the mare and rushed forward. Were there bodies in the ashes? He could not tell. He saw the badly burned remains of his chain-mail armor, probably damaged beyond use. No matter, he never wore it anyway. But where was Tall One?

"Heads Off!" Coyote shouted. "Come! It is Tall One's time for birthing!"

The little man was picking his way among the debris. "She and Eagle are with us in the woods. She says to tell you that your elk-dog medicine is safe!"

The wonderful girl, Heads Off thought, tears of relief in his eyes. The enemy attacking, she in labor, and taking time to save Lolita's Spanish bridle bit because it was her husband's most important symbol of strength, the elk-dog medicine.

18
>> >> >>

As they hurried toward the shelter of the broken, rocky ravine, Coyote rapidly sketched the happenings of the morning.

It had not taken long to realize that the village was extremely vulnerable, with all of the horses and most of the young warriors gone. The remaining warriors, realizing the possibility of a trap, had organized a defense. Coyote modestly played down his own very important part of the plans, but Heads Off was aware of it. Coyote could introduce an idea and make others believe they had thought of it.

As luck would have it, the most experienced group in the old ways of run-and-hide fighting were now in charge. The Bowstrings moved the women and children into the broken, wooded area, and prepared for the expected attack.

The wait was not a long one. Fifteen or more mounted warriors thundered into the area from the north, yipping their war cries. A shower of arrows left several horses riderless, and the bowmen retreated toward the ravine. Riders wheeled in pursuit of running men on foot, and several of the People fell before the survivors gathered at the mouth of the gully.

Protected by rocks and trees, they now made a stand. Every attempt at approach by the enemy horsemen was met by well-aimed arrows from ambush. For a time it appeared that the Head Splitters were considering an attack on foot, but they abandoned the idea, probably as too costly.

So, a stalemate resulted. The Head Splitters could not further pursue the People, but the People could not move from their hiding places.

Frustrated, and knowing that the Elk-dog warriors would be returning, the enemy turned again to the empty village. They looted the lodges, fired a great number of them, and mutilated the few dead of the People. They were just starting to withdraw when their scouts called out the approach of the returning Elk-dog men. Insolently, the enemy mounted and rode over the ridge to the west.

Heads Off was greatly tempted to pursue and punish, but realized the futility. He beckoned to Long Elk.

"Get the others, and catch any loose elk-dogs. Stay near!"

Long Elk nodded, and swung to his horse, shouting to several others of the young men.

Tall One lay in a small clearing ringed by berry bushes. Big Footed Woman stood proudly by. Heads Off hurried forward.

"It is finished, my husband," the girl announced proudly. She lifted a corner of the robe to show a round red face against her shoulder. "We have another small man-child!"

Heads Off knelt and touched his wife's face, squeezed her hand.

"The child is beautiful," he told her. He was still numbed by the great risk they had just survived.

"No, not beautiful, but big and strong," she answered, smiling. "Here, hold him!"

Heads Off lifted the carefully wrapped bundle and peered at the owlish face.

"He is healthy? Well-formed?"

"Yes, my husband, but he has no fur."

The little group chuckled together. It was a family joke. At the time of the birth of Eagle, Tall One had been extremely depressed that the newborn had no facial hair like his father.

Heads Off nodded solemnly.

"Yes," he answered, "it is too bad. Shall we try until one has fur on his face?"

Coyote chuckled happily, and the baby blinked his large eyes at the brightness of the day.

"I think he should be called the Owl," announced Coyote. The name would stick longer than anyone knew. Coyote was extremely perceptive when it came to names.

Another, temporarily deferred, thought struck Heads Off. He knelt beside his wife.

"Tall One," he began, hesitating, "our lodge is gone."

"I know, my husband. I saw it start to burn. It is no matter. We had none before our marriage. Now we will have another."

Heads Off wished that he could be as matter-of-fact about possessions as the People. Their home, all their food supply, all had gone up in greasy black smoke, and ". . . It is no matter." He knew better. It would be a very hard winter. It must be spent here, at this place, with little food and worse, with little chance to hunt.

The Head Splitters now knew their weaknesses. In fact, they may have known all along. Increasingly, Heads Off began to suspect that they were engaged in a sort of cat-and-mouse play, with all the advantage on the side of the enemy.

"You will move in with us, of course." Coyote was talking. "We have plenty of room."

It was not "plenty," Heads Off knew, but would be adequate, though crowded.

"What will the rest do?" he asked his father-in-law.

Coyote shrugged. "Move in with relatives. Not more than half have lost their lodges." He spoke as if this were good fortune.

The People were scattering down the stream, returning to the ruined camp. Coyote and Heads Off turned to follow and evaluate the extent of the damage.

"See if you can find my cooking stones!" Tall One called after them.

People were already sorting debris, salvaging even unburned portions of smoldering lodge covers.

"They started with the biggest lodges," observed Coyote.

It was true. The enemy had deliberately selected the lodges of the more affluent on which to wreak destruction. This lent more weight to the thing Heads Off feared. It had been a deliberate move to destroy supplies and to destroy the ability to obtain more, by reducing the horse herd.

The high wailing of the Mourning Song rose from the far side of the camp as someone discovered the loss of a family member.

Standing Bird trotted up, astride his red buffalo mare.

"We have several more elk-dogs, Heads Off!"

"It is good!" And there's not much that is, he added silently to himself. "Tie them all, so we lose no more. And, Standing Bird," he called as the other reined away, "spread word of a council tonight. We must make plans."

There was much to do before dark. The People moved like ants, meticulously working over the ruined debris of their homes. It was found that the empty make-believe lodges had been spared, probably because they appeared makeshift and worthless. Soon they were no longer a pretense, but actual homes of the dispossessed. Others did indeed move in with relatives.

One amazing thing had occurred. The lodge of White Buffalo was untouched. Even though one of the most pretentious, and therefore most subject to attack, the enemy had left it intact. The medicine man was taking credit for the omission, pointing out that he was protected by the strength of his medicine. Most of the People readily accepted this interpretation of the matter.

Heads Off knew that his friend and adviser, White Buffalo, was an opportunist, taking advantage of a situation to increase his prestige. However, it seemed likely that the enemy had indeed avoided damage to the lodge. They could easily recognize it as the lodge of a medicine man, by the intricate and extensive painting on the lodge skin. Not knowing the extent of this man's powers, they would avoid direct confrontation as a matter of safety. So, in effect, the young chief realized, the old man was correct. His medicine, or at least the fear of it, had saved the lodge of White Buffalo. And, the sacred white cape of the People was still safe.

Bodies of the dead were ceremonially wrapped by mourning families, and prepared for transport next day to tree scaffolds for burial. The enemy dead and wounded had been carried away by their comrades as they departed.

All was far from complete as Sun Boy finished his daily run, but other activity came to a halt as the council fire was lighted. The People began to straggle to the center of their ruined camp.

19
>> >> >>

Despite the urgency of this council, the customary amenities were observed. Heads Off had long since come to understand that such serious matters as council must not be hurried. Still, he felt the press of time as he lighted the pipe and blew puffs to the four directions, to the sky and to the earth. He passed the pipe to the sub-chief on his right, and sat back to wait as the instrument made its circle.

Finally, the circle was completed, the pipe stowed away, and the discussion could begin. Coyote took the cased council pipe from the chief. He was very proud of his daughter, the Tall One, for having the presence of mind to pick up the chief's pipe and his elk-dog medicine as she fled. These objects were practically all that had been saved from her lodge, but they were most important.

"Let us count the dead," Heads Off was speaking.

A general accounting was discussed. There were apparently four dead, all males. This indicated good organization in the defense and retreat, but was grim news in light of the already thin ranks of fighting men. One had been a mere boy, eager to display his bravery, but too inexperienced to compete with hardened warriors. Even so, an older warrior testified, the youth had stood fast and shot an arrow which unhorsed his opponent.

"I saw the Head Splitter fall, but I do not know if he was killed," finished the man.

"How many Head Splitters were killed?" the chief asked.

No one knew. Estimates ranged from three to seven, with a median figure probably most likely.

"There was one still alive," a man related. "We found him hiding in the rocks and killed him."

Heads Off was furious. He would have wished to question the prisoner, to see how much the Head Splitters might know of their plight. He was also wondering if the attackers were of the band of Bull's Tail. He had an accurate estimate of the size of that group.

"Let us not kill prisoners before they are questioned!" The irritation in the chief's tone was unmistakable.

There was another factor here, too, understood but incompletely by the chief. Coyote had already observed it. Traditionally, the People were much likelier to adopt a prisoner than to kill him. Now, with the stress of internal strife and the threat of the enemy, the easy-going attitude of the People was changing. Their first thought was to lash out, to kill. Coyote hated to see this change come over the tribe. Almost, he thought, it was better when life was simpler, and we thought more of run-and-hide.

The council continued. It was determined that everyone had a place at least for the night, and then Heads Off outlined plans.

"We have no more than twenty elk-dogs."

"No, my chief!" interrupted Standing Bird. "Nearly thirty!"

The elk-dog men had found several strays, including mares, foals, and animals once ridden by Head Splitters who had no further use for elk-dogs now.

"It is good," Heads Off acknowledged, "but still, we cannot move camp without more elk-dogs."

A flurry of discussion followed. The People, it was noted, once moved entirely without elk-dogs, using only the power of their muscles and that of their dogs.

"That is true," observed Coyote, "but it was before the

elk-dog. We now have bigger lodges, and longer poles. Dogs and people cannot move the lodges we now have."

"But, the biggest were burned!" someone insisted.

"My chief," interjected the medicine man, "there is a wintering place that the People used long ago, not more than three suns away. We should be able to move that far. We also need food. There are deer in the woods, and nuts among the trees. It would be better for the winter than this place."

There were nods of assent. Others remembered the location, now unused for many seasons. Under Hump Ribs, the previous chief, the band had migrated farther south to winter. In addition, they had become more dependent on the buffalo in recent years. With the advent of elk-dog hunting methods, buffalo were more accessible. No one ate dog meat now except by choice, and rabbits and squirrels were hunted mostly by the youngsters.

Now, it seemed advisable to revive some of the old ways. In fact, this might be the only answer for the band. Ultimately, it was decided to spend another day in salvage and burial, and then make the move on the following morning.

It was a ragtag remnant of the proud Elk-dog band that straggled out onto the prairie two suns later. Heads Off had insisted on mounted warriors flanking the column. Yet at the same time, the strength of the men was needed to drag and carry. Stops were frequent and progress slow.

Tall One insisted on walking part of the time, carrying small Owl. Frequently, however, she consented at the urging of her husband, to ride for a time on a pole-drag behind one of the horses.

There was a time of fear when one of the outriders sighted a mounted warrior watching from a distant hill. No further such observations were made, however, and by dark there was much doubt and discussion as to whether the young man had actually seen anything.

"But, my chief, there *was* a rider!"

The scout had come to the cooking fire where Heads Off sat eating. He had been derided and laughed at, and was becoming depressed.

"I know," the chief nodded. "The Head Splitters will surely be watching our move. You," he flattered the youngster a little, "are simply a better watcher than most."

The young man left, immeasurably helped by the encouragement.

"That is good, Heads Off," Coyote observed. "It will make him a better scout."

"I spoke truth," answered his son-in-law. "We know the Head Splitters are there, but only this young man has been able to see them. He may some day be as good as Sees Far!"

Midday of the fourth sun the Elk-dog band straggled into the area they sought. Heads Off rode ahead to evaluate and select a campsite. It must be judged both from the standpoint of winter shelter and from that of defensibility.

In the former case, he saw the selection was excellent. The level camp area was ringed on two sides by a steep and broken hillside. It would protect from the north and west, good shelter against Cold Maker. A dense patch of hardwood timber to the south promised shelter for the animals, as well as nuts and small game for provisions.

To the east, the fringe of oaks thinned out to a narrow neck of ground which opened onto the prairie. Defensibility against a mounted attack was adequate, against infiltration through the woods, not quite so desirable. This was partially offset by a nearby hill which would present a good location for a sentry.

Heads Off rode to that point, a few hundred paces away, and was pleased. A single observer, protected by the blankness of open prairie behind him, could overlook the entire area. It would be next to impossible for the enemy even to infiltrate the woods unobserved. He beckoned with a full-armed sweep, and the band filed into the little meadow to select lodge sites.

The next days were busy, almost frantic with activity. Lodges were erected and insulated with dry grass stuffed inside the linings.

While the leaves of the oaks and walnuts in the grove changed to gold and orange and crimson, the prairie grasses ripened to muted shades of red and buff. Prairie flowers of gold and purple showed their spectacular glory.

It was the Moon of Ripening, sometimes called the Moon of the Hunter by the People. The significance of the Hunter's Moon had been somewhat diminished with the change to hunting buffalo with elk-dogs. Now, both names took on added significance. The People, who had been moderately well supplied for the winter, now found themselves with practically nothing. The Head Splitters had been thorough. Most supplies had been looted or burned.

Nights were cool and crisp, the days pleasant and sunny, deceptively comfortable. Younger members of the band, including the chief, were filled with a complacence that the elders found alarming. There were those who remembered when the Moon of Hunger in late winter was marked by starvation. Already, long lines of calling geese were to be seen in the sky, making their southward journey. It would not be long before, in a short blaze of crimson, the sumac on the hillsides would suddenly drop foliage and the Moon of Falling Leaves would begin.

Cold Maker would sweep out of the north, pushing Sun Boy and his torch far to the south. White Buffalo watched the signs, shook his rattles and danced his ceremonial dances. He, with others of the older generation, saw the coming season with dread. He could remember no time when the People were so poorly prepared for the onslaught of Cold Maker.

20
>> >> >>

There were many among the People who remembered the Hunger Moons in winters before the elk-dog. These were the ones who impressed upon the younger members of the band the urgency of the situation. The gathering of food was an absolute necessity for survival. Without it many of the People would face starvation before the Moon of Greening.

But there were more difficulties. The buffalo, now the staple of the People, had already migrated farther south for the winter, leaving only small scattered bands or lone outcasts. They might be encountered by accident, but an organized large scale hunt was completely impractical. Especially, Heads Off thought grimly, with so few elk-dogs as they now possessed.

Attention turned to the older methods, and youngsters who had never known hunger helped gather some of the old foodstuffs now scorned by the affluent People. Hackberries, their sweet thin layer of fruit scarcely worth the effort, were gathered by the children. They were pounded, seeds and all, into a coarse sticky mash, to be mixed with dried meat and tallow for winter pemmican. Nuts were plentiful, of several varieties. Some were cracked and the rich kernels kneaded into the mixture. Other nuts were simply stored in the shells.

There were large quantities of acorns in the woods, and someone recalled that in hard times gone by, they had been utilized as food. The secret was to boil the bitter kernels repeatedly until all the acid was leached out. The mealy remains could be dried, or mixed with dried meat for storage.

Squirrels were plentiful. Youths who a few moons ago would have scorned such small game now spent much time stalking with bow and arrow. Rabbits, likewise, became an addition to the everyday fare of the People.

Some of the band reverted to the old custom of eating dogs, but the medicine man attempted to discourage this practice. It was not that White Buffalo objected to the use of dog meat. He enjoyed a fat haunch of roast dog as much as anyone.

"But the dogs must be saved," he scolded. "They can be used in the time of snows when times are hard."

A few ignored the medicine man's warning, but most of the People agreed. There would be no easier way to obtain fresh meat in the Moon of Snows. Perhaps, no other way.

The pitiful piles of provisions grew slowly. Sometimes it seemed that despite all the industry the band was showing more supplies were consumed than were gathered. The volume of meat supplied by the kill of large animals such as buffalo was sorely missed. Heads Off began to wonder if a short foray onto the plains might not be an answer. If a few buffalo could be found, it would provide great benefit.

He spoke to Coyote, who was very cautious.

"I do not know, Heads Off." He shook his head. "The Head Splitters may be waiting."

Irritated by the resumption of run-and-hide thinking, the young chief still had to admit that his father-in-law was right. He had once made the near fatal error of dividing his force. He must not do so again. The safety of the band depended on his decisions.

Tall One had recovered her strength rapidly. The owl-eyed infant, who already seemed to possess the wisdom of the ages, was rapidly gaining size. Owl was more solemn and reserved than his smiling and outgoing older brother. The big dark eyes, so like those of Tall One, his father noted, seemed to observe and consider all things. It was almost as if, Heads Off reflected, the infant realized the dangers of having been born practically in the heat of battle. He wondered idly whether this would make the child a great warrior. Then he smiled to himself. His thought processes were becoming more like those of his wife's people all the time. Anyway, this tiny infant already appeared to be more a thinker than a warrior. How early a child's personality makes itself known, he thought.

He looked around at their older son, Eagle, playing actively with a small bow and arrow. The youngster had indicated without a doubt that he preferred this activity to that of gathering nuts.

The gaze of Heads Off lifted to the sentry on the hilltop. It had been decided to keep a lookout constantly on watch. Piles of brush had been prepared, to be lighted as an alarm at a moment's notice. So far, there had been nothing to report.

The young chief himself had taken his turn at the lookout. To do so was actually against his background and training, but there were several reasons.

He wished to be completely informed, and could remain so more easily if he were a participant. Their numbers were limited and his presence would make things easier on the other warriors in turn. He also felt that active participation would ensure the continued respect of the younger warriors.

When he got right down to ultimate reasons, however, Heads Off knew why he chose to stand his turn at lookout. Even as a cadet, the long hours on sentry duty had been not unpleasant for him. The hours of darkness just before dawn were his favorite time to be on lookout. There was time to think, to enjoy the quiet of the prairie, quiet yet busy with a myriad of little night sounds.

Finally the blackness in the eastern sky would fade to pale gray, then yellow, and the incomparable beauty of the prairie sunrise would unfold before his eyes.

It was on such a morning a few suns later that Heads Off sighted something of importance. It was not quite full daylight yet, just the tip of Sun Boy's torch showing above earth's rim.

He was watching the earth sleepily come alive. Below him in the village, smoke of cooking fires was beginning to rise from the apex of some of the lodges.

A great blue heron stood in a quiet pool of the stream beyond, head cocked to one side and still as a statue, waiting for a movement in the water.

A dog yapped lazily. A man came out of his lodge, yawned and stretched, and walked around behind the lodge to urinate. To watch the quiet peace of the pastoral scene below, one would never guess that within a few moons this band might easily be fighting for survival. Fighting against Cold Maker, against starvation, and quite possibly, against the enemy. The Head Splitters must know their predicament now, and also know where they were camped for the winter. He had been somewhat surprised that there had been no overt attack since they retreated into these makeshift winter quarters.

At the thought, he swept the horizon with his gaze for one more of many times. He stopped short at a hint of distant movement to the north, attention fixed.

Through a distant pass between two low hills, he could see something moving. He studied for a few heartbeats, and verified his impression. The deliberate, casual nature of the motion told him that there were animals, grazing animals, on the prairie. He thought of buffalo, but the pattern was wrong. Horses?

No, he saw, as the big animals grazed closer and became close enough for color to be distinguished. Not buffalo, or horses, but elk!

In some places almost as numerous as the buffalo, elk ranged in loose, far-spread herds across the prairie. This appeared to be a large group, slowly moving almost directly toward the camp. Anxiously, Heads Off watched as the animals straggled slowly through the gap and spilled out across the plain. This herd, he realized, might make the difference in survival for the People.

One major problem nagged at him. The behavior of elk did not permit hunting them efficiently from horseback.

Elk were swift and agile, and would not run straight away from a horse, as buffalo did.

A hunt on foot, using the old methods, must be quickly organized. He slipped down the hill and hurried into camp.

21
>> >> >>

The hunters lay hidden in the grass, among scrubby
bushes along the rimrock. The elk moved closer in a
leisurely manner. Heads Off gripped his lance and tried
to relax for the interminable time of waiting. He had
chosen this weapon in preference to the bow, as he was
more familiar with it.

The older hunters of the Bowstring Society had taken
great pleasure in organizing the hunt. *Aiee*, it was like
the old days! Rapidly but cautiously the hunters were
deployed in a long arc along the broken, rocky crest of
the hill. Part of the skill involved was that of guessing
which way the drifting elk herd would move. Now it
appeared that the judgment of the Bowstrings was good.
The elk were moving directly into the desired area.

White Buffalo had given them a favorable vision, though
he admitted his medicine was better with buffalo than
with elk.

The horses had been left at the village. Odd, thought
Heads Off, crouching against his limestone rock. The
People have had horses only a few years, and already it is
common knowledge: buffalo are easily hunted on horse-

back but elk are not. No one would even consider a run with a lance at one of the big deer.

The herd moved closer, and Heads Off tried hard to remain perfectly motionless. An ant crawled across the toe of his moccasin, across its upper rim, and onto the bare skin of his ankle. The tickling sensation was almost more than he could bear. Yet he must remain still. The existence of the entire Elk-dog band of the People might depend on it. The food represented by the herd now approaching could easily make the difference in survival or starvation in the Moon of Hunger.

He could now see movement through the thin screen of sumac bushes in front of him, and the ant was forgotten. An old cow elk, apparently the leader of the herd, was picking her way carefully across the flat hilltop. The others straggled behind her.

The position of the hunters had been chosen carefully so that the slight breeze would be from behind the animals, toward the men. This would prevent their discovery until the last moment.

But now, with the leading animals well within the curve of the hunters' hiding places, stray puffs of wind might give the alarm at any time. Already the old lead cow was nervously looking around, head high and nostrils flared. Behind her, a yearling male snorted nervously, and a huge bull with a magnificent set of antlers raised his head to investigate.

Heads Off was so intent on watching that he was not even aware of the first shot. The hunters were to wait until Big Bow released the first arrow, and then all would shoot at once. The spearmen would rush in from the sides of the arc, attempting to head off as many animals as could be turned back again toward the bowmen.

The yearling bull suddenly sank to his knees and rolled over on his side, kicking feebly. Heads Off realized that the shooting had started only when he caught glimpses of other flying shafts, and the elk began to mill around in confusion. Another animal went down.

Hunters from the far wings of the arc sprang forward, shouting and waving robes. The herd split, part of the animals retreating the way they had come, and the others turning back into the circle of bowmen. They were met with another flight of arrows.

A fat cow rushed almost directly at Heads Off. He readied his lance for the impact, but at the last minute the elk turned. He made a futile thrust, missed, and turned his attention to a large bull that thundered past him. Heads Off evaded the swinging antlers and thrust again. The lance was ripped from his grasp, leaving him weaponless. Another elk rushed toward him, and he waved his arms and shouted to turn the animal back toward the hunters.

It was all over very quickly. Three elk lay still in the dry grass of the prairie. Several other wounded animals limped or staggered away, the hunters in hot pursuit. The women began to arrive, laughing and chattering, to start the butchering. Someone handed Heads Off his lance. He did not know whether it had been taken from a dead animal or if it had fallen from the wounded bull as it fled.

He looked around at the number killed, and was somewhat disappointed. It was good, much better than nothing, but not as successful as he had hoped. They would need much more meat.

Heads Off saw some of the hunters returning from the chase, unsuccessful. Perhaps, he thought, a wounded animal or two could be pursued on horseback. He beckoned to Long Elk and Standing Bird.

"Let us bring the elk-dogs. We may find another kill or two."

Soon the three were mounted, moving back out onto the prairie in the direction taken by the retreating animals. Within a few long bowshots' distance, they found a dead cow elk with an arrow's feathered end jutting from her flank. They rode back far enough to signal the others, and then swept in a wide circle, looking for signs of any other wounded.

It was Standing Bird who first saw the bright splash of blood on short dry grass. They picked up the track, finding just often enough, another spot of crimson to mark the trail. The wounded elk was traveling rapidly, but they passed one spot where it had stood for a little while, steadily dripping blood. They pushed ahead.

Still, Sun Boy had passed the overhead position before they spotted the animal. It was a large bull, and from all appearances, even at a great distance, he was tiring rapidly. The hunters hurried on.

The bull was lying down when they approached, but leaped to his feet and staggered away, with the three in hot pursuit.

So great was the excitement of the hunt that they became oblivious to all else for a time. Unnoticed was the fact that they had pushed rapidly away from the rest of the band. Also, a change in the weather was brewing. The gentle puffs of wind had swung around and stiffened to a steady breeze. By the time the lances reached their target and the elk went down for the last time, the day had become almost windy.

The hunters dismounted, and began to discuss the problem at hand. They were far from the butchering party, and the meat must be cared for immediately.

"My elk-dog will carry," offered Standing Bird. "We can cut the meat into pieces we can load."

The others nodded. If necessary they could walk and lead the horses. They fell to work. The elk was quickly gutted, and the head removed. It was more difficult and time-consuming to disjoint the quarters and prepare to load the resulting haunches on skittish horses. Sun Boy's torch sank lower in the sky. Finally they were nearly ready to depart.

"*Aiee!*" exclaimed Long Elk, pointing. "Look!"

Along the horizon stretched a series of columns of dense gray smoke. Even as they watched, the smoke thickened and became more prominent, rising to obscure a large part of the sky. It seemed only moments later that the first acrid smell reached their nostrils. The prairie was on fire, the flames fanned by the brisk southwest breeze.

"Leave the meat! We can ride around the fire!" The young chief began to untie the thongs.

"No, Heads Off! It moves too fast!"

Heads Off looked again, and saw that the smoke now presented a solid front across the distant prairie. In places the leaping flames could already be seen. Worst of all, the rushing front of fire stretched so far across the horizon that there could be no hope of moving around the end of the blaze. There appeared to be no end.

A distant crackle could now be heard, and the horses

began to fidget nervously. Flecks of powdery ash flew past on the wind, and the smoke smell became stronger. Tongues of flame licked high into the air, higher in some places than the tops of the willows along the winding creek beds.

Momentarily, Heads Off wondered how the fire had started, but rapidly dropped that line of thought. The important thing was survival. He looked around for a body of water, a hill with little or no grass, or a steep bluff that would stop the onrushing inferno. No such feature presented. Anxiously, he turned to his companions.

Standing Bird was fighting to hold the now excited horses. Long Elk, however, looked as calm as if no danger at all presented. He was squatting calmly nearby, scraping with his flint knife on a couple of sticks.

Heads Off did not know whether to laugh or be angry. Had the young man completely lost his senses? He started to question, then decided against it. Long Elk was a highly intelligent young man, rivaling his father, the Coyote, in practical sense. Perhaps he had a reason for his seemingly illogical actions.

The sticks, Heads Off noticed, were from a nearby yucca, the dried pithy stems of old bloom stalks. One had been flattened and the other partially sharpened at each end, like a spindle. Could he, possibly, be making rubbing sticks for starting a fire? The young chief's thoughts whirled. Was there some medicine-thing of the People about *stopping* a fire with fire sticks? Nothing in the ways of the People surprised him any more.

Fascinated, he watched as Long Elk cut a stout green stick from a bush nearby, and began to trim it. Heads Off glanced anxiously at the now rapidly approaching wall of flame. Whatever Long Elk was working on would certainly have to be effective. The horses danced and pulled against their reins, eyes rolling apprehensively.

Long Elk now calmly untied his breechclout and dropped the skin to the ground. With the thong, he fashioned a bowstring for his green stick. Yes, Heads Off decided, he was making fire sticks! Long Elk twisted a turn of the string around the spindle, and placed the pointed end in a depression in the other yucca stick. A stone with a natural socket fit neatly over the upper end of the spindle.

Heads Off had seen fires started in this way many

times since he joined the People, but never under such tense circumstances. Long Elk squatted and twirled the spindle with an experimental stroke or two of the bow, then began to stroke in earnest.

With the first few turns, white smoke began to rise from the fire sticks, then a small pile of brown charred powder began to grow near the tip of the spindle. More strokes of the bow, and the tiny pile of rubbed powder seemed to glow like an ember. When he saw this, Long Elk dropped the sticks and carefully began to breathe on the glowing spark, finally picking it up on a handful of fine dry grass to blow gently from underneath. Suddenly the bundle of grass burst into crackling flame and Long Elk quickly thrust the burning brand against a clump of dry grass beside him.

Fanned by the wind, flames licked across the nearby tuft of tinder-dry vegetation. In a few heartbeats Long Elk's fire was spreading rapidly downwind, growing in breadth as it ran.

Long Elk rose, retrieved his thong from the fire-bow, and donned his breechclout again. He tossed the fire sticks aside and reached to take his horse's rein from Standing Bird. He led the animal to the area where his fire was now dying back, the hot leading edge already racing up the opposite hill. He stepped cautiously on a dying blaze or two, and then led his horse onto the bare and blackened ground.

"Come," he said. "We can go now."

22
» » »

The three hunters gingerly led their skittish horses across the warm and still-smoking ground. After a few hundred paces, Long Elk stopped, and they turned to watch the wall of fire as it raced up behind them. Darkness was falling, and the eerie yellow light of the flickering flames made Heads Off think of stories of Hell from his childhood.

The racing fire swept closer, and its noise became a roaring, increasing in intensity as it descended. A pair of rabbits, crazed with fear, darted past them and into the hazy dusk. Even at this distance they could feel the heat of the flames. To Heads Off, in his first encounter with the awesome might of prairie fire, the thing seemed alive. It was an evil, malevolent monster, intent on their complete destruction.

The fiery wall seemed to concentrate on the huddled figures, rising in intensity as it neared the point they had recently abandoned. The awesome blaze seemed to tower over them for a moment as its full force crashed against the edge of Long Elk's backfire. Then, falling back in frustrated fury, the wall of flame split in two, sweeping around them to the right and left.

Heat and roaring sound faded in the distance as the fugitives stood coughing and wiping their eyes in the dense smoke. The frantic horses began to quiet somewhat. The air was clearing, and occasionally a scrap of sky shone through a rift in the curtain of smoke above them.

"We should wait," suggested Long Elk, "for enough stars to find our way."

Calmly, he squatted in a position of rest, and relaxed.

It was full dark before the drifting smoke had cleared. The wind had died. The three men could see, in the far distance, the long line of fire snaking across the rolling prairie.

They had said little during the time of waiting. To open one's throat produced a spasm of coughing. Each, however, had done much thinking, along the same general lines. Each was thinking of the village, and how their families had fared.

There was little concern for their escape from the fire. The butchering party was near enough to the campsite to retreat there. The camp itself was protected by the circle of trampled and close-grazed grass around it. What small fires might approach could be easily stamped or beaten out, and if necessary, backfires would have been lighted.

The one gnawing concern in the mind of each was the same: had the village been attacked? It had become apparent that someone had fired the dry prairie. It was sometimes known for prairie fire to start from lightning, but there had been no storm. Therefore, human hands must have applied the torch.

And, who would benefit from the burning of the prairie? In the Moon of Greening, the People often set fire to last year's grass to hurry the growth of new grass and attract the buffalo to the lush green. The medicine man observed and carefully supervised the timing of the ceremony. But this was entirely the wrong time of the season. No one of the People could possibly benefit from the blackened and scorched landscape.

Therefore, the conclusion was inescapable. The fire had been set by the Head Splitters. Was it for the purpose of a diversion so that an attack could be launched?

As their lungs cleared, the three began to discuss the question, and found that all had the same fears. They must return quickly.

The stars were now visible in the still smoky sky, and they oriented themselves by the Seven Hunters and the Real-star. Long Elk pointed a general direction and started ahead, leading his elk-dog. The others followed.

The blackened world around them presented a strange and eerie landscape. Here and there a flicker of flame still sparkled. An occasional buffalo chip smoldered, producing a ghostly white wisp of smoke against the charred black background.

The time seemed endless until they finally reached a hilltop which enabled them to see the campsite. To their great relief, everything seemed calm. The dull red glow from cooking fires inside the lodges was a reassuring and comforting sight. The camp had not been attacked.

They hurried forward, raising a long shout as they came near, to be sure they were not mistaken for enemies.

The People, they found, had managed to divert the fire. They had chosen a place several hundred paces from the camp, where natural features would assist them. A small rocky creek bed, though dry, had provided a place to set backfires. A fortunate shift in the wind at the proper moment had helped. With only a little effort at beating out stray tongues of flame, the main force of the fire had roared past to the west.

Everyone was jubilant at the successful maneuver. White Buffalo, of course, was modestly taking some credit for the shift of the wind. The grass near the camp, needed for the elk-dogs during the coming moons, had been saved.

There had been concern, of course, for the three missing hunters. Again, however, the concern was not only for their ability to escape the fire, but the enemy.

Heads Off embraced his wife, who laughed at his smudged and blackened face. Her concern was apparent, however, as she brushed at his cheek.

"Did you see any Head Splitters, my husband?"

He shook his head.

"No. None came here?"

He handed her the rein and lifted the grimy bundles of meat from the mare's back. Big Footed Woman cuffed

the dogs away and started to work with the bundles, and
Tall One joined her.

Heads Off led the mare around the lodge and to water
at the stream. Coyote fell in beside him and walked in
silence for a time. Finally the young chief spoke.

"What does it mean, Coyote? Why did they fire the
grass?"

Coyote shrugged. "Who knows why Head Splitters do
as they do?"

"But this would have been the time for them to attack!"

Coyote nodded. "They would fail to attack only if they
had not enough men."

Slowly, the thing began to make sense. It was apparent
that the Head Splitters had known all along where the
band had camped for the winter. They had so far avoided
an open attack. Not since their defeat in the Great Battle
had the enemy dared that.

But now, they had an opportunity. A weakened band of
the People, isolated and low on provisions, could be
observed for the proper moment to attack. It would be
impossible to maintain a large force nearby to observe,
but a scout or two might easily watch and report the
actions of the People.

The enemy scouts, seeing the People scattered over the
prairie for the elk hunt, had been unable to resist the
opportunity to harass them with fire. Lacking the strength
to attack, they could still make much trouble.

With this new understanding came a feeling of dread.
Heads Off could see no way that the band could move.
They would be under constant observation. Under threat
of attack at any moment, they would dare not leave the
protection of their present camp. Even hunting parties
would be vulnerable to raids by the superior forces of the
enemy.

The noose was tightening slowly but surely around the
Elk-dog band. They had been lucky today. At the next
encounter, they might lose a warrior or two. A sentry
might become careless and fall to an arrow out of the
darkness.

Heads Off could almost follow the thoughts of the
enemy now. Not wanting to risk a frontal attack, they
would harass, weaken, and starve the People until the
proper time.

He thought of a scene he had once witnessed on the prairie. A group of wolves had encircled an aged buffalo bull. Once the sheer strength of the animal would have prevented their considering an attack. Now, old and weak, his reflexes slowing, he was making his stand. One wolf, then another, dashed in to harry and snap at the old monarch's heaving flanks. He whirled to meet each rush, only to be attacked again from another quarter. It was only a matter of time until the bull would go down for the last time.

Heads Off had, in a sentimental gesture, chased the wolves off with his lance. But, he knew they would return.

Now, he felt a close kinship to the old bull. The Elk-dog band of the People were in a very similar situation. They might fend off the minor attacks, might escape the prairie fire, possibly even avoid starvation through the winter. Eventually, though, would come the final rush.

Heads off could see no other ultimate outcome. Sooner or later, they would be overrun. It seemed highly unlikely that the Elk-dog band would ever move from the spot where they now wintered.

23

>> >> >>

In the days that followed the fire, the People of the Elk-dog band became more relaxed and happy. The weather was uncommonly fine. Sun Boy's torch shone with warm beneficence, and as the leaves ripened and fluttered slowly to the ground, it seemed that all was well with the People.

Much elk meat had been salvaged, and the women were busily preparing it for storage. The elk skins, also, must be dressed and tanned. It was a comforting return to a semblance of normality among the band.

But Heads Off was worried, and was joined in his concern by Coyote and White Buffalo. The People were far too complacent. There was not enough food for the winter moons, and though many realized it, they seemed unconcerned. The easy affluence of the past few winters had lulled the People into complacence. Only the older members of the band remembered hard times and starvation. The younger ones seemed to expect that something would happen without effort on their part.

Yet an even greater concern was felt by the young chief. He had now become sharply aware that the Elk-dog band was under observation. The Head Splitters might not maintain a continuous watch, but it was discomforting to know that they were out there somewhere, waiting. The People could never be sure whether, at any given time, they were watched or not. It mattered little. Sooner or later, the attack would come. Heads Off was inclined to think the enemy would wait until the Moon of Greening, when the People would be further weakened by starvation. The greening time was a favorite time for raiding by the Head Splitters. The opening of the weather in springtime caused restlessness among the young men.

So, in his own mind at least, Heads Off had formed this definite idea. The major attack would be in the spring. In the meantime, the enemy would make their presence known from time to time, to prevent the People from moving about freely to hunt.

The problems of the band, then, were two in number. That of winter survival was most immediate, but there remained the other need. A plan for defense of the village must be devised. Heads Off studied the geographic features of the area from the top of the lookout hill. His mind wandered back to his studies at the academy, so far away now. As Cadet Juan Garcia he had been instructed in such things, but had never been a good student. He kept thinking in terms of Roman defenses, walls and barricades and buttresses. There had been pictures in some of the books in the academy library.

But, the People had neither the manpower nor the equipment to build earthworks. Their best efforts could do little more than pile flimsy barriers of brush around the lodges. This had been done for many generations, to break the force of the wind and to catch the drifting snow.

Heads Off began to see that such a barricade might be useful across the narrow place where the meadow opened onto the prairie. It was there that the charge by yelling horsemen would come. Any barrier to slow the thundering rush of the enemy would be helpful. He envisioned such a brush device as he studied the area below him. Yes, it would slow the charge, as horses paused to jump and riders found it necessary to give full attention to their mounts for a moment. Now, if he only had a hundred foot-lancers to hide behind such a barrier! The charging enemy could be decimated by a well deployed force.

But, he sighed, he had no squadron of lancers. There were only the thinned ranks of the People. The older, more experienced warriors were bowmen, needed to defend the flank against enemy on foot, attempting to infiltrate through the trees.

Their few skilled lancers were young men of the Elk-dog Society, those who had not followed the rebels. They would have little opportunity to mount a counterattack on horseback in the cramped confines of the village. It would probably be necessary for them, also, to fight on foot.

Aiee, if they had a hundred pairs of hands, if only to hold spears. Slowly, an idea, born of desperation, began to dawn. Yes, it might work! He hurried down to explain his plan to Coyote.

In a frenzy of activity, the People began next day to cut and drag brush for the barrier. Heads Off could imagine the unseen watchers of the enemy chuckling at the futile efforts of the doomed band. Such a flimsy barrier could be easily jumped by charging horsemen, even pushed through.

In fact, Heads Off was carefully supervising the construction personally. He did not want the structure too high or too wide. It must invite the overconfident enemy warrior to jump his elk-dog over the barricade. There lay the potential success of the plan.

Along the inner edge of the brush barrier lay hidden a deadly surprise. Sharpened poles, propped at an angle and camouflaged by thin brush, jutted to meet the enemy. Dozens of these make-shift spears of varying heights were concealed along the barrier, forming a defense almost as effective as the squadron of lancers the chief had wished for. Better, perhaps. This plan had the additional element of surprise. Heads Off felt a resurgence of confidence.

Soon came the night when Cold Maker swept down on the camp. Icy rain pelted on the lodge skins, making the distinct drumming sound now familiar to Heads Off since he joined the People. The smoke-flaps were tightly closed and the Elk-dog band settled in for the storm to pass.

Next morning icy crystals sparkled on the trees, brush, and the grass of the prairie. The few remaining leaves dropped quickly from the trees along the stream. Only the majestic oaks in the grove retained their foliage. Previously turning a warm red, the oak leaves now became dead, curled, and brown, but would cling tightly to the branches, until replaced by new growth in the Greening Moon.

The importance of this quality of the oaks was, for the People, the shelter they provided. Shelter, not for the People, but for the occasional deer that might find their way into the area. They would become potential food for the lean moons.

The People proceeded with their preparations for the winter, optimistically deferring thought of the coming conflict.

Their predicament was sharply recalled one crisp afternoon when two small children ran screaming from the grove where they had been gathering firewood. Warriors seized weapons and ran to their defense, to find nothing.

Nevertheless, the children insisted that they had encountered a heavily armed Head Splitter. The man had sprung at them with a horrible grimace as they dropped their sticks and fled.

There were those who were inclined to discount the entire story. The children, it was said, had vivid imaginations, and had been frightened by a shadow or a deer in the dark woods.

"What do you think they saw?" the young chief asked his father-in-law in private.

Coyote was slow to answer. "I am afraid, Heads Off, that they saw a Head Splitter."

The young man nodded. This fit the pattern he had envisioned. The enemy would show himself just enough to keep the People alarmed and under stress. They would be unable to pursue, or even to organize a hunt for food outside the environs of the camp itself. This incident was a clear message. Even the woods were not safe. The noose was tightening around a doomed band of the People.

Heads Off again felt that he had failed in his responsibility to his wife's people. What would be said at the Sun Dance next year, he wondered? There would be an empty place in the circle of chiefs at the Big Council.

24
>> >> >>

The winter was not exceedingly harsh, but neither was it entirely mild. There were several storms, when Cold Maker roared across the prairie, spreading his thick robe of white behind as he passed. Sun Boy, though pushed far to the south, fought back each time. The rays of his torch warmed and melted the drifted snow and in a few days it was possible again to move cautiously around the immediate area.

There was no imminent danger of attack at this time. It would be far too dangerous to travel. The Head Splitters would not risk being caught in the open by a whimsical thrust on the part of Cold Maker. Besides, the enemy would be well aware, Heads Off reflected grimly, that the People had nowhere to go. His diminished band had no alternative course. They must merely sit and wait, attempting to conserve their scanty food supply, and wait for the inevitable attack.

One old woman apparently cracked under the stress. It was a gray afternoon, with Cold Maker's heavy dark clouds moving threateningly from the northwest. Soft flakes of snow were already falling, and the People were hurriedly gathering the last few sticks and chips for the cooking fires before withdrawing into their lodges.

Three children came running from the fringe of trees along the stream.

"Rabbit Woman has walked into the prairie!"

The woman had been gathering sticks with the youngsters, they related, and had moved somewhat farther down the stream. Suddenly, she stopped, carefully placed her little bundle of fuel on the ground, and walked away, singing to herself.

"Show us where this happened," demanded Heads Off.

The children led a group of warriors and anxious relatives to the area.

A pitiful pile of sticks lay mutely on the ground beside the trunk of a massive old cottonwood. The searchers peered into the gathering gloom of the storm, but no moving figure could be seen. The wind was rising, and snow fell more thickly. It would be out of the question to organize a search with darkness coming on and Cold Maker howling for victims.

Coyote addressed the children, who stood wide-eyed and frightened, peering into the snowy dusk.

"What was Rabbit Woman singing?"

"It sounded like the death song, Uncle."

Coyote nodded, and laid a comforting hand on the shoulder of the small girl. Through the mind of Heads Off flitted the words of the death song.

> "The grass and the sky go on forever,
>   But today is a good day to die."

The strange haunting song was used seldom, only when one felt that death was imminent. Occasionally a warrior would sing it in battle, as an indication that he intended to fight until he died. Heads Off felt it strange indeed that an old woman would use the death song at this time.

"Come," said Coyote, "let us go home."

The little group solemnly turned and shuffled back toward the lodges.

"Bring the firewood," Coyote said to the children. They divided the little pile of fuel and followed, each carrying a small burden. Heads Off fell into step beside Coyote.

"Rabbit Woman went mad from the worry, Uncle?"

'Coyote looked sharply at the young chief, then spoke gently.

"No, Heads Off. It is one of the old ways of the People. Rabbit Woman gives herself to the prairie, so there will be more food for the young."

They walked on in silence. Heads Off now began to understand the old woman's use of the death song. It was her way of fighting for the survival of the People. Just as a warrior might sing as he gave his life in defense of the tribe, Rabbit Woman had gone proudly to her death, singing.

> "The grass and the sky go on forever,
> But today is a good day to die."

She had performed the ultimate sacrifice for her people. Heads Off would think of this brave woman's contribution many times during the coming moons.

As food became scarcer, the People became thinner and weaker. The best of the available provisions were assigned to the children. This, Heads Off had learned, was the way of the People. The younger generation, the hope for the future, must be preserved at all costs.

Eventually, supplies dwindled until most of the band was relying on the dogs. There had been a time when Heads Off had thought he would never be hungry enough to enjoy dog meat. Now it proved a quite acceptable staple.

Still, by the end of the Moon of Snows, even dogs were becoming scarce. The Moon of the Hunger promised to live up to its name. Remaining supplies were carefully hoarded, to be parceled out as necessary. Some families, less prudent than others in the use of their supplies, began to suffer.

Occasionally, the desperate situation would be eased by a deer kill as an isolated animal wandered into the area looking for a place to winter. However, by the Hunger Moon the animals were no longer moving around. It would be extremely unusual to have more opportunities to obtain venison.

Animal parts that would have once been discarded or tossed to the dogs now became a source of subsistence.

Thin, watery soups boiled from hide and offal at least filled bellies for a short while.

Still, the situation was becoming desperate. There were scarcely enough dogs left to reproduce, although the possibility of enough future for the Elk-dog band to need such foresight seemed remote.

"Heads Off, we must eat the elk-dogs." Tall One whispered as they snuggled for warmth in their sleeping robes one night. She had placed her children in their robes after a very meager meal. Owl, of course, still fed at breast, but she was afraid her milk was diminishing. Heads Off had given special attention to her nutrition, contriving ways to give her part of his own food. She loved him for it, but it was not enough. The girl knew that she was losing rapidly. Owl cried for more when she had given him all the milk her undernourished body could produce.

Her husband held her tightly.

"I know." He hated the decision. Not only were the esthetics of eating horse meat foreign to his upbringing, there were other considerations.

The great changes in the culture of the People, which had come about in such a short while, were totally derived from use of the horse. The use of the elk-dog had enabled so many advantages that it was questionable if the People could return to the old ways.

To be more specific, suppose that they ate the elk-dogs to survive the winter. Suppose further that by some miracle they were able to withstand the onslaught of the Head Splitters in the Moon of Greening. With no elk-dogs, how could they hunt? And, equally important, if they had eaten the elk-dogs, there would be no way to replace the animals. Some breeding stock must be preserved, at all costs.

Ultimately, however, the decision must be for day-to-day survival. A council was called, and the matter discussed. The animals would be sacrificed one at a time, as needed. First would be the geldings, incapable of reproduction. Heads Off held the vain hope that before all the neutered animals were used, something would occur that would save the mares, and the foals they might be carrying.

The first of the horses was slaughtered the next morning. At least, for a time, bellies would be full, and children would not cry out in the night from hunger. When this food was gone, the next animal would be sacrificed.

As it occurred, however, only two of the elk-dogs had been slaughtered before events of overriding importance changed the situation completely.

25
>> >> >>

The day came, as the People knew it must. The look-out on the hill first spotted the approach of the enemy. He raised a long cry and lighted the signal fire as a warning to all, before he retreated to the village.

The Head Splitters were in force, more in number than three men have fingers and toes. They paraded arrogantly, circling and wheeling their elk-dogs in mock combat on the open prairie beyond the brush barricade.

But there was no attack. All maneuvers stopped well beyond range of a long bowshot. They spent most of the day showing themselves and their strength, and then calmly made camp a few hundred paces down the stream. Heads Off rankled in sheer frustration. Briefly, he considered a sortie after dark, but quickly abandoned the idea. It would never do to risk even a few warriors. All would be needed in the final attack.

The People carefully posted sentries in the woods to prevent a sneak attack by infiltrators on foot, and retired for the night. Heads Off slept little. He could think of no other course of action that they might take now. There was nothing but to wait. Still, how hopeless the plight of the Elk-dog band seemed. Again and again, he blamed himself for poor leadership. Why had he ever consented to act as chief?

It was shortly after full daylight that the charge came. The enemy had been charging and wheeling in insolent display when suddenly a semblance of order emerged out of the milling mass. Apparently at a shouted signal, every Head Splitter reined his horse around. The ground shook with the thunder of hundreds of pounding hooves as they swept down on the ill-equipped People.

Elk-dog men seized weapons and sprinted toward the flimsy brush barricade.

"Watch the woods!" Heads Off shouted. This might be a diversionary attack.

The mass of yelling enemy continued to thunder down on the village, their falsetto *"yip-yip-yip"* swelling in the morning stillness. Now they were almost within bowshot. A few nervous defenders loosed arrow shafts, only to see them fall short.

Suddenly the charging mass wheeled, turned, and came to a stop, laughing, pointing, and joking among themselves. They rode slowly back toward their camp, leaving the defenders limp and frustrated. Heads Off quickly looked for another point of attack, but there was none.

The enemy had simply withdrawn. Then the young chief began to see. It had been merely a feint, a bluff, to place the People under further stress. The Head Splitters were playing with the doomed village, twisting their fears and doubts. He remembered a cat that he had watched toying with a mouse, long ago in his childhood so far away. The enemy were merely enjoying the opportunity to wreak slow vengeance on the People. Again, he despaired that any would survive to leave this campsite.

For the rest of the day, the People remained on the alert. Everyone carried weapons, and the Head Splitters were constantly watched.

No remarkable events occurred. Several times, a handful of the enemy would ride close to the brush barricade, but stop just short of bowshot. They appeared to be mostly eager young men, who contented themselves with shouting challenges and obscenities. They were obviously under instructions not to engage in actual contact. The young warriors of the People could not refrain from answering the taunts, but managed to restrain themselves from any overt action.

A young man of the enemy rode near and shouted at the defenders, punctuating his words with sign talk.

"We will kill you, and then your women will learn how to bed with real men!"

A single arrow arched from the camp of the defenders, hung high for a moment before falling short. The Head Splitter laughed.

Long Elk answered for the People. "I see no real men. I see only cowards who are afraid to come within bowshot!"

The exchange of insults continued through the day at intervals, but both sides knew that it was just talk. The situation remained unchanged. There was little sleep that night, but no attack came.

Next morning, the Head Splitters carried out another mock charge. The terrifying rush again terminated just short of bowshot, and ended in laughter, jokes, and obscenities toward the defenders. The ritual was repeated the following morning, and the People began to relax over the lack of any follow-through. Coyote, White Buffalo, and others cautioned not to become careless.

The following day the enemy changed tactics somewhat. Daylight showed no massing of armed horsemen. The People, alert for trouble, nevertheless started about their morning routine. Women took waterskins to the stream, and cooking fires produced their hanging layers of white smoke above the lodges.

Suddenly a woman's voice rose in indignation.

"*Aiee!*" she shouted. "The water is fouled!"

It was true. Others tasted their waterskins or cupped a hand to the stream. Once clear and sparkling, the creek was a murky, muddy gray-brown in color.

It was easy to see the situation. The Head Splitters had simply taken their horse herd upstream and held them for the night in or near the water. Heads Off could recall the flat grassy meadow which they had probably utilized. Now the water was fouled with particles of mud and bits of manure. The situation was becoming more desperate.

The People were experienced in scarcity of water from past dry seasons on the plains. They methodically scooped shallow basins in the sandy streambed, and allowed seep-

ing water to fill them. At least it was wet, and the taste
was better than that from the stream itself.

Heads Off, chewing on a tough stringy strip of horse
meat that evening, was afraid that the solution to the
water problem had been too easy. The enemy would
continue to herd their elk-dogs upstream, and the water
would become worse. He could imagine how the constant flow from above would pollute every back-eddy.
The stench, in a few days, would become unbearable,
and even the seep water undrinkable. If, indeed, any of
the People were still alive in a few days.

The daily massed charge still occurred, but the time
now varied. Sometimes it was shortly after first light,
sometimes when Sun Boy stood high overhead. Once it
was when the last fading rays from Sun Boy's torch
threw long shadows across the plain. It appeared that the
enemy realized the effectiveness of unpredictability.

To add to the stress, a sentry was killed in the woods
one night. The young man was struck down so quietly
by the telltale war club that it was not until morning
that his body was discovered.

The event produced more sleepless nights. It was easy
to imagine that everyone was individually under the
observation of the Head Splitters. In the mind's eye, it
was easy to see an enemy face peering from every shadow.
The People became more depressed, and a feeling of
helplessness settled over the camp.

26
>> >> >>

At last the day arrived when the actual charge came. The enemy had massed their wheeling, shouting ranks as usual, while the defenders watched, weapons at hand. The horsemen whirled and thundered in the noisy charge straight at the barricade. The high yipping falsetto of their war cry echoed across the plain.

The front ranks of screaming warriors reached the point of bowshot range, where they always turned back. But today, they only increased speed and thundered on. Men of the People shouted and rushed toward the barricade.

"*Aiee,*" Coyote muttered softly to Heads Off at his elbow, "today they come!"

"The woods! Watch the woods!" Heads Off yelled. Several running warriors turned and sprinted toward the edge of the timber.

But there was no attack there. The entire mass of yipping horsemen were massing the attack against the barricade. Heads Off watched, fascinated, as the front ranks neared the flimsy wall of brush.

A big bay with a yelling warrior on his back pounded along in the lead. This would be the first animal to reach the jump. The horse tucked his forefeet neatly and cleared the brush at a low point. Suddenly, what should have been a graceful landing turned into a grotesque nightmare. One of the sharp stakes, still unseen by the attackers, plunged into the body of the big horse and he went down, the rider thrown violently over the animal's head.

In the space of the next heartbeat, elk-dogs all along the line of brush cleared the barricade and impaled themselves on the waiting spears. The yipping war cry of the Head Splitters was drowned in the screaming of stricken horses and men. Dying animals floundered and kicked, rolling on injured riders. In turn, the next wave, moving too rapidly to stop, cleared the jump, only to fall and tumble as they tripped over struggling, plunging wounded.

Warriors rushed forward, shooting, spearing, clubbing the wounded enemy. Few of the attackers managed to strike a blow. Most who were still able clambered frantically across the damaged barrier to escape, followed by a hail of arrows. Heads Off saw a throwing stick whirl from the ranks of defenders, and bounce smartly off the head of a retreating warrior. The women were joining the fight. The Head Splitter somersaulted forward off the barrier and was lost to sight.

Mounted Head Splitters who had managed to stop before their elk-dogs made the jump wheeled to pick up unhorsed comrades. In a few more moments the whole thing was over. The Head Splitters were in full retreat.

Heads Off still stood numbly, half sick at the destruction his tactics had caused. His horseman's instinct rebelled at the loss of fine stock. Still, first things must come first.

"We did it!" he breathed, half to himself. "We stopped them."

A ragged cheer rose from the beleaguered camp. Some of the youngsters had to restrained from chasing after the retreating Head Splitters.

Warriors moved along the barrier, making sure the fallen enemy presented no further threat. A few confused elk-dogs, saved from major injury by having fallen over the bodies of their stricken companions, wandered inside the brush wall, calling frantically. Several badly wounded animals were quickly destroyed.

An old woman shuffled forward, butchering knife in hand.

"The Head Splitters have brought us meat!" she cackled merrily. Her flint knife fell to work at the task of skinning.

Others joined in the butchering, and in a short while the village appeared remarkably as if there had been a successful hunt. Strips of horse meat were strung on the drying racks, and even the skins were pegged out like those of buffalo.

A celebration began to take shape for the evening hours. True, there was little to celebrate, and the respite was only temporary, but after all, it was a victory of sorts. The enemy had been stopped.

The Head Splitters, for their part, had withdrawn to their camp, still within plain sight of the People. They seemed confused and enraged. Apparently the People's defense had been a complete surprise. About midday, a group of three Head Splitters were seen to mount and ride away across the plain, finally disappearing in the west.

"They go to tell the others," Coyote stated simply.

Realization had begun to sink home to Heads Off already. The Elk-dog band of the People was little better off than before. They still could not move from their present location, could not hunt, could do nothing but wait for the end.

Again, he considered the possibility of an attack on the camp of the enemy war party. Now would be the time, with a sizable number of their warriors killed or wounded, and many of their elk-dogs dead.

But, he reflected, the fighting status of his own band was even worse. They had only a handful of young warriors trained in the use of elk-dogs and lances. It would, of course, have to be a horseback attack. An encounter on foot would make them completely vulnerable as they approached the enemy across the open plain. The foot warriors would be cut to pieces by mounted enemy.

Even with the Head Splitters in temporarily weakened condition, the People could not risk an attack. The enemy would soon bring reinforcements, each new warrior hot for revenge.

Equally out of the question was the thought of attempting a move. The band was seldom more vulnerable than when on the move, even under the best of circumstances. They could be easily trapped in the open, encumbered by the women and children and all the miscellaneous baggage that represented the life of the People.

Now, at weakened strength and with few elk-dogs, the band would be as helpless as an orphan calf before wolves.

For a short while, Heads Off considered a move in desperation. If they left all their belongings, lodges, poles, everything, and took only food, they could move more rapidly. Everyone must take all the food he could carry.

But if they were pinned down by the enemy in the open plain, they would be unable to move at all. There would be no way to replenish the thin supplies of food and water. They would have only increased their vulnerability. He discarded the plan, at least for the present. There were more pressing things to think about.

The bodies of the enemy dead were dragged outside the barrier. Young men repaired and reinforced the damaged portions. There was no need to replace the sharpened spears which had been broken or torn away by the thrashing bodies of dying horses. They would no longer be effective. Now that the enemy was aware of this device, he would not try the same frontal attack again.

Heads Off wondered idly where the next attack would come. Through the woods, probably.

27

>> >> >>

The People rested well, tired from the hard day's activity as well as the impromptu celebration and dance. There was no danger of attack from the disorganized enemy.

Sun Boy's first light revealed that the bodies of the enemy dead were gone. They had been carried away in the darkness. It was important to the Head Splitters to save their honor by recovering their dead. The bodies would be mourned, wrapped in robes with their most valued possessions, and placed on burial scaffolds much like those of the People.

The Elk-dog band, meanwhile, continued to exhibit a sense of triumph, almost of euphoria. The People had lost not a single life.

They had more supplies than a day ago, and had dealt the enemy a telling blow. It was easy to become overly optimistic about their situation.

Of course, tradition of the People lent itself to a sort of day-to-day existence. If there were no food today, well, maybe tomorrow. Heads Off had at times become very impatient with this cheerful optimism. In his own culture, it would have been considered childish, overly simplistic. He had once spoken to his wife about this general attitude.

"But what is there to do?" Tall One seemed puzzled. "We do what we can, and be ready for whatever happens next. Something always does."

Yes, he had thought grimly, something always does, even if it is bad.

It was impossible today, however, to remain glum and concerned. The mood of the People was contagious, happy with the victory, and Heads Off found himself smiling, laughing. It seemed not to matter that the band still could not move from this campsite. It was enough for now that they had food, and that in the distance could be seen the furious, frustrated enemy, milling aimlessly around their camp.

The day was marked by uncommonly fine weather. It was one of the warm, earth-smelling days which occur in the Moon of Greening. Heads Off sought out his wife, and the two climbed part way up the hill behind the lodges, to sit in the warm rays of Sun Boy's torch. Since the loss of their own lodge, privacy had been very difficult to achieve. They had missed not only the close physical intimacy, but the opportunity to share time together, to exchange thoughts. It was good, sometimes, to be in the warmth of the family in Coyote's lodge, but it was very crowded. There were times when privacy was needed more than the companionship of the extended family.

Heads Off saw, among the curling grasses of the previous season, a scattering of tiny ivory white flowers. He stepped over and picked a few of the blossoms, bringing them to the rock where they sat. Tall One held the tiny cluster close to her face.

"The Dog Tooth," she smiled. "Do you remember, you brought them to me in our first springtime together?"

He had hoped she would remember, and he was pleased. It had been before the birth of Eagle, before Heads Off had been burdened with the responsibility of leadership. Things had been so much simpler then.

He sat close to her and they watched the activity in the village below. The appearance was that of a peaceful, prosperous band of the People. Children played, meat

vas drying on the racks, and skins were stretched to
dress and tan. Women called to each other at their work,
with occasional laughter.

Only if the couple on the hill lifted their gaze to the
prairie beyond, could they see that all was not as well as
it seemed. There they could see the milling, impatient
activity of the Head Splitters.

"They will come again, with more warriors," the young
chief spoke grimly.

"Of course. But not today." She snuggled closer against
him.

Heads Off never ceased to be amazed at the manner in
which this slim girl could make him completely forget
all the problems of his existence. When he was in her
arms, nothing else mattered. All was right with the world,
and there could be no wrong.

Later, he sought out his father-in-law.

"Coyote, how long until they come again?"

Coyote shrugged. "Maybe three suns, maybe ten. It
will be when the others gather. This time they will be
very strong."

And they were certainly very strong before, thought
Heads Off desperately. There had been far more than
enough warriors to crush the dwindling Elk-dog band.
His defense had worked only because it was so unortho-
dox, so unexpected. It would not be successful again, and
he had no more tricks in mind. At least, the threat of the
sharp weapons in the brush barricade would prevent the
main attack from coming that way. If only there were
some way to make the woods more defensible.

They established a general line of defense in a zigzag
pattern through the thickest part of the timber. At the
insistence of the chief, each warrior chose his position,
that to which he would hasten when the attack came.
Some of the women, too, stated that they would fight
beside their men. Piled brush helped to take advantage of
natural variations in the terrain.

A few men would remain at the brush barrier where
the horsemen had perished. There was likely to be a
diversionary attack there, too.

Some families selected hiding places for their children,
to which they would run when the fatal day came.

Then, there was nothing to do but wait. Time hung

heavy over the People. For some it was a time of quiet, private thoughts. For others, a time of smoking and telling of tales.

There were those who passed the time in gambling. At several places around the camp area could be seen a cluster of people intent on the roll of plum stones. The painted stones skittered and bounced on spread skins, and much property changed hands in wagers. The gamblers, it seemed, were ever so much more serious in their gaming. In spite of the threat of annihilation that hovered over them, they were intent on the games. Wagers were high, at times most of a man's possessions riding on the toss of the plum stones. There seemed to be an almost frantic preoccupation with the games of chance.

Well, why not, thought Heads Off as he walked among the lodges. It may not be that any of us have any possessions·in a few suns. When life becomes cheap, property becomes even cheaper.

More depressing to him, somehow, was the sight of the women, busily engaged in preparing skins for future use. The tedious, long-drawn-out task would eventually produce usable robes, garments, and lodge covers. Despite the fact that there was little likelihood of anyone in the Elk-dog band ever enjoying the use of the end product, the work went on. Women who took great pride in their work continued to dress and scrape hides meticulously.

Other women worked to construct garments and moccasins that would never be worn. But, the young chief sighed, what else was there to do? All activity would not stop because the future seemed unlikely. He turned back to his own family's lodge, to encounter the most heart-rending sight of all.

Tall One sat cross-legged near the doorway of the lodge, sewing ornamental quillwork on a pair of tiny moccasins. She held them up for his inspection.

"They are for Owl's First Dance," she announced proudly.

A child's First Dance, at the age of two, was an important step in his life. It was the time of the naming ceremony, when an older relative would choose the name the child would wear until grown. The finest of garments, the most careful of grooming, the most intricate of ornamentation on moccasins were a matter of great pride to the family.

Now, Tall One worked a complicated and beautiful design with dyed quills into the surface of the tiny shoes. They would truly be objects of beauty. Owl could stand proud in the dance arena in the carefully sewn garments made by his capable mother.

Except, thought Heads Off dully, except for one thing. For small Owl, chortling there on the robe in the warm spring sunshine, there will be no First Dance.

By that time, there would be no Elk-dog band.

28
>> >> >>

It was five suns before the first of the newly arriving Head Splitters came. There were six or seven of them, and they lost no time in circling the camp of the People.

An arrogant young chief, resplendent in his war paint, charged alone to within a bowshot of the barrier. He pulled his big horse to an openmouthed, sliding stop, while several young warriors of the People hooted in derision.

Heads Off, however, did not like the serious, business-like way in which the other looked over the situation. Here was a man who was accustomed to having things go his own way. He apparently intended to see that they did.

More enemy warriors arrived next day, and still more the next. For several suns, small groups of Head Splitters trickled into the area, to mingle with those already there. They seemed in no hurry, were willing to wait for the proper moment.

Each morning a handful of enemy warriors, always the same individuals, would ride out and exchange taunts and derision with the young warriors of the People. It seemed a half-hearted, boasting attempt to goad each other into an indiscretion, and was completely unsuccessful.

Still, the strength and number of the enemy increased. It became evident that there were warriors arriving from several different bands of the Head Splitters. This seemed to indicate that word had spread among that tribe. All who wished vengeance for the defeat in the Great Battle a few seasons back could now gather. It was a deliberate, almost ceremonial preparation that the enemy was now making, for the extermination of the Elk-dog band of the People.

The Moon of Greening was now nearly past, and the Growing Moon beginning. It was time to start the journey to the Big Council, but no one mentioned that fact. It would have taken most of the Growing Moon to make the move. The tribe would gather at a prearranged site on the Salt River, starting the Sun Dance and Big Council in the Moon of Roses.

Again, Heads Off thought of the circle of chiefs at the Big Council. There would be an empty space this year, and for all the years to come. It would be pointed out to future generations that the empty place in the circle had been that of the Southern, or Elk-dog band, exterminated long ago by the Head Splitters. There would be a record of the event painted on the Story Skins and preserved in the history of the tribe. It would be remembered for all time as the year the Elk-dog band was killed. Oddly, he wondered how the painters of the skins would depict the scene. Even at such a time, the hope crossed his mind that the Elk-dog people would be portrayed as dying bravely and fittingly. Then he shrugged. What did it matter?

Heads Off watched the enemy as they moved around their camp from day to day, hunting and practicing with their weapons. Once a party of Head Splitters made a buffalo kill within sight of the People. They made a great exaggerated show of butchering and preparing the succulent hump ribs, knowing that the captive band was near starvation, and subsisting on the tough, stringy meat of the elk-dogs.

One of the recently arriving groups of Head Splitters had actually brought their lodges and families with them.

Such confidence was beyond belief. It was unheard of to take women and children on a war party. The only explanation, of course, was obvious. The conclusion of the events now approaching was foregone. There was no danger involved, the enemy was saying, in merely exterminating this helpless, starving band of the People. The arrival of the families of Head Splitter warriors meant simply contempt for the beleaguered People.

There was one slim hope that kept occurring to the young chief. With all the warriors of different bands now gathering, there seemed to be a lack of organization. With his previous military training, this was more obvious to Heads Off than to the others.

When they had been confronted by only the one enemy band, there had been a semblance of order. The mock charges, the attack that was to have been final, had all been organized and well-disciplined. Now there seemed, at least from this distance, to be mere milling confusion. There appeared to be no directed effort to organization on the part of the enemy.

Heads Off discussed this with Coyote and a few of the others.

"I think you are right, Heads Off," Coyote nodded thoughtfully. "They have lost some strong chiefs in the attack. No one is their main chief now."

"How can we use this?"

There was a long silence, then Long Elk spoke.

"We could have attacked while they were weak," he said wistfully.

"No, they were not that weak. It was too dangerous." Heads Off was firm.

They continued to discuss the situation, but could arrive at no conclusion. It would require a major surprise to take advantage of the enemy's disorganization. Something like an unexpected attack, and the People had simply not enough strength for such a move. They had only a few elk-dogs and a handful of young warriors trained to use the lance on horseback. The only way such a group could be used was in a suicide charge. Then there would be even fewer warriors to withstand the final onslaught. Heads Off refused to consider such a plan.

In the final event, the enemy was so overwhelmingly

superior in numbers and equipment that it would matter little how disorganized they were. What matter if the defenders were sliced efficiently to pieces, or merely crushed in a disorganized trample?

29

>> >> >>

"**C**ome, my friend," Coyote was speaking. "Let us go and speak to White Buffalo."

The two men threaded through the camp toward the lodge of the medicine man. It was now the most pretentious lodge remaining, the only one of the big lodges constructed in recent years. Heads Off wondered what would happen in the final debacle. Would the lodge of the medicine man fall and be destroyed with the rest, or would the enemy's strange fear of his medicine spare it again?

It was entirely possible, he decided, that the enemy would leave the medicine lodge as the only thing standing, and its occupants the only living things on the scene when they departed.

"Uncle!" Coyote was tapping on the taut lodge skin. "We would speak with you!"

Crow Woman held aside the door skin and the two stooped to enter. The delicate scent of dried herbs assailed their nostrils as they stepped into the dusky interior and greeted the medicine man. He was seated in the host's place directly across from the doorway, solemnly smoking. He nodded and motioned them to sit.

"Uncle," Coyote began, "we wish to speak of the Head Splitters."

White Buffalo nodded again and sat, still not speaking.

"Could you," Heads Off spoke at last, "tell us of the coming fight?"

The old man turned and stared wearily at him for a long moment. Then he sighed, and rose to collect the various accoutrements of the dance that would help his vision. Crow Woman warmed the drum over the fire to tune it, and started the rhythmic beat. The fixed expression on her lined face left no doubt that she considered the situation hopeless.

Heads Off had always been impressed with the ritualistic dances and visions of the medicine man. To be sure, White Buffalo was an opportunist. The old man was a shrewd observer, watching the actions of animals, birds, and insects, as well as the patterns of the weather. He was acutely aware of human behavior as well. By the use of all the information available to him, White Buffalo's vision predictions were remarkably accurate.

Heads Off had sometimes been amused by the way in which the medicine man took credit for fortunate happenings. White Buffalo's shrewd powers of observation allowed him occasionally to guess the outcome of the course of events, slightly before they were seen by the others. Thus he could foretell or warn and seem to predict correctly things yet to happen.

These were the thoughts that drifted through the mind of the young chief as they watched the dance. The intricate preparation, the face-painting, the costuming and manipulation of the scepterlike gourd rattles. But Heads Off, watching the old man, had the feeling that his heart was heavy. White Buffalo, more than anyone, had the insight to see the ultimate outcome of the events in progress.

Heads Off began to feel sorry for the medicine man. The band had long looked to him for advice. His visions were usually optimistic, sometimes with a warning if necessary. But now, when the conclusion of this siege was clearly to be tragic, what could the medicine man say? There was no way the old man could give an encouraging forecast. Heads Off wondered if it were possible for him to present a bleak vision.

Possibly White Buffalo was thinking of the same dilemma. There was something of depression and despair in the shuffle of his feet, the slope of the shoulders and swing of the head.

At last he finished the dance and Crow Woman spread the painted skin on the floor of the lodge. Perhaps it was only in the imagination of the onlookers that the incantation was a little longer and more fervent. White Buffalo made his cast, and bits of bone and wood and pebble skittered and skipped over the surface. As they came to rest, the medicine man began his interpretation.

"*Aiee!*" he muttered to himself. He glanced quickly at the others, something akin to excitement and genuine surprise in his face.

"What is it, Uncle?"

The medicine man seemed puzzled. He poked the bright pebbles gently with a gnarled forefinger, muttering to himself. The suspense was growing intolerable.

"It is good!" he finally exclaimed, the expression of surprise and bewilderment still on his face as he rocked back in a squatting position on his heels.

"But, Uncle," Heads Off interjected, "how can this be?"

The medicine man shrugged, as if such things were beyond his powers to interpret.

"I only know that the signs are good!"

The uncomfortable thought struck Heads Off that perhaps the old man's mind had snapped from the stress. How could any sign be good? Still, the confident expression on the medicine man's face, his calm demeanor, and the alert look in his eye were not those of a lunatic.

It was difficult not to become caught up in the obvious mood of White Buffalo. No further information was forthcoming, however. He had said all he would. That was the message that his prediction had to tell.

"The signs are good."

It was obvious, as Crow Woman placed the equipment of the dance back in its place, that the interview was over. White Buffalo resumed his seat, and relighted his pipe. Coyote and Heads Off thanked him and Crow Woman held the door skin aside for them to leave. Already there was a change in her face, optimism beginning to shine through.

Possibly it was Crow Woman who spread the word. At any rate, it traveled like a prairie fire. By the time they reached their own lodge, people were calling to each other the cheerful message.

They encountered Big Footed Woman at the door.

"What is it, my husband?"

"White Buffalo says the signs are good!" Coyote sounded puzzled.

His wife lifted her glance to the gathering of the enemy camp beyond the brush barrier.

"But how can this be?"

Both men shrugged again, still bewildered. A long shout reached their ears from down by the stream as someone called to a friend.

"The signs are good."

It was impossible not to become caught up in the optimism of the thing. Even Heads Off began to believe, against what he knew to be true. By dark he, too, was completely convinced that by some miracle they would be successful. Though outnumbered three to one, the People would turn the enemy back at the barricade and emerge victorious.

Just what would happen next was unclear. How they could escape from the siege remained a mystery. Yet the new optimism was contagious. Everyone had a new strength and determination, despite the fact that nothing had changed. The mere message "the signs are good" had transformed the spirit of the band.

The People retired that night with more hope than they had had for many suns.

And it was that night that the enemy burned the barricade.

30

>> >> >>

Heads Off awoke at the first cry of alarm from one of the sentries. He sprang from the sleeping robes and grabbed his lance as he dashed outside, ready to defend the lodges.

But there was no attack. A flicker of light from the direction of the brush barrier made him turn that way. There was a warm spring breeze from the southwest, and as it struck his face, it carried also the unmistakable smell of fire. He trotted upwind, zigzagging among the lodges, and came into the open of the meadow just as someone gave a long shout.

"*Aiee!* They are burning the brush!"

Flames were licking hungrily through the tinder-dry barricade in at least three places. No enemy were to be seen. They had planned well. Under cover of darkness they had chosen the proper moment to creep to the barrier and ignite it. Fanned by the brisk breezes, the fire was already burning well out of control. Several people were silhouetted against the glare.

"Stay back! Let it burn!"

There was no hope of extinguishing the flames anyway, and to approach the light of the fire was to invite an unseen arrow from the darkness.

The People gathered in groups to watch the destruction, staying well back to avoid a chance bowshot. A few warriors, at the suggestion of Heads Off, trotted to the woods in case of an attack from that direction. Coyote thought that event highly unlikely. The Head Splitters were known to avoid combat at night. According to their beliefs, it was said, the spirit of a warrior dying in the night was doomed to wander forever, lost in the darkness.

Whatever the reason, no major attack by the enemy had ever occurred during night time. They might strike at a lone sentry, or steal elk-dogs, but not engage in battle.

So it was with some sense of temporary security that the People watched their major defense burn. Heads Off, however, was thinking rapidly ahead. This event would require a complete reevaluation of their defensive position. Obviously, the enemy would now have easier access to a charge by horsemen.

By first light, the chief was on the hillside with a few warriors, to assess the new situation. He doubted that the attack would be immediate. The enemy, too, would need to evaluate the changed condition.

As he had feared, the destruction had been complete. The wind had died, but where the defensive barrier had been was now only a strip of smoldering gray ash. An occasional wisp of smoke still rose from an incompletely burned log. Even the remaining sharp stakes had been burned off at the ground. There was nothing at all now to stop or even slow a charge by the milling horde of horsemen beyond.

"Can we rebuild it?" Standing Bird spoke.

Heads Off shook his head.

"No, there is not time. They will come as soon as the embers are cool enough to ride over."

In addition, the supply of available brush was becoming scarce. Much had been used for fuel during the winter, and more for the barricades in the woods.

As if to add to their worries, a soft rain began to fall, obscuring their view of the enemy camp beyond. The men started back toward the lodges. No one spoke, but the thought was present. The light spring rain would cool the embers more rapidly and facilitate an enemy attack. Already a curtain of steam was rising from the hot ashes, giving the illusion of an ethereal defensive barrier, the ghost of that now destroyed.

The downpour was becoming heavier, and they scattered to their respective lodges.

Heads Off had seen all he needed. The main attack would now come, he believed, sweeping in from the prairie through the meadow, now unobstructed, for a massive crushing charge. There might be a diversionary attack through the woods, but it would be the force of the enemy horsemen that would need to be reckoned with.

He struggled to devise a solution to the defensive problem. Some of the positions in the woods could be filled by those women skilled with weapons, but there would still not be enough warriors. They were still outnumbered by at least four or five to one.

"Uncle," a small girl, Coyote's youngest daughter, spoke hesitantly, "could we stop the Head Splitters with ropes where the barrier was?"

For a moment, the idea looked valid. By knotting together all the rawhide lariats in the village, it might be possible to string a line or two across the narrow isthmus.

Then reality returned. The first charging elk-dog might be slowed, perhaps even trip and fall, but that impact would also break the rope. It was simply impractical. He patted the child on the head.

"We might try it, Snowbird," he smiled. Inwardly, he wondered if this handsome girl would grow up to grace the lodge of some enemy warrior as his slave-wife.

The rain continued through the day, but shortly after dark the stars began to appear. There was all the promise of a bright warm day to come. Almost without thought, the People seemed to know that tomorrow would come the battle, the last for the Elk-dog band.

No one had any inclination to sleep. They wandered uneasily about the camp, greeting friends, preparing weapons, making final plans and preparations. In grim anticipation, there were jokes about how many Head Splitters each warrior must account for in the battle.

Their defense plan was pitifully simple. The women and a few of the warriors would station themselves in the woods with those children old enough to use weapons. They would hope to stop whatever attack came on foot from that direction. There were enough who had skill with the bow to handle this assignment, Heads Off felt.

He would personally lead the mounted warriors. On horseback they would form a living barrier across the now undefended meadow. When the charge came, they would attempt to slow the oncoming rush so that the Bowstrings, stationed on each side, could make themselves felt.

"We must strike as many as we can very quickly," he cautioned. "If their numbers are smaller, we have a chance to fight. Try to kill those who appear to be the leaders first."

He could convince himself, almost, that it was possible. If they could, very early in the conflict, even the odds somewhat . . .

31

» » »

In the gray light before the dawn, the People made their last preparations. Older women herded small children together to retreat to the broken hillside for hiding. Tall One kissed her children and handed Owl to Crow Woman. She spoke to Eagle, old enough now to understand the gravity of the situation.

"My son, if you are captured, always remember that you are of the People, and be proud!"

She turned and picked up her bow and quiver of arrows. Taking the Spanish bit from its peg, she placed the thong around her husband's neck.

"You must wear this, Heads Off. It is our strongest medicine."

She kissed him softly, and looked long into his eyes.

"Go now, my husband. Remember, White Buffalo says the signs are good!"

He had almost forgotten that. Now, in light of the progress of events, he was ready to scorn the prediction.

Coyote, carrying his bow, gave his son-in-law's hand a quick squeeze.

"We will be there to strike when you need us," he said simply. "The signs are good!"

Heads Off could not speak. His eyes were filled with tears as he returned the little man's grip and quickly turned to his gray mare.

The horsemen gathered in the open area before the lodges. Even though he knew they were few in number, he was shocked. The People were able to mount fewer than a score of warriors. He could see the men of the Bowstrings slipping on foot to their respective areas of concealment in the gray light of dawn.

A figure came up beside the gray mare. It was White Buffalo.

"Heads Off," he called. "I have cast the stones again." The old medicine man still seemed puzzled. "It is the same! The signs are good!"

"Thank you, my friend," Heads Off smiled.

He reined Lolita around to face the open prairie, flanked by Standing Bird and Long Elk. Every face was ceremonially painted. The small band of horsemen moved slowly forward, watching the enemy camp. Sun Boy's torch was now peeping above earth's rim, and visibility was improving rapidly.

In the distant camp, a flurry of activity was evident. Heavily armed, painted enemy warriors were swinging to their mounts and calling to each other as they assembled. There were too many to count.

Heads Off led his Elk-dog warriors to a spot just short of the ashes of the barricade. It would be important to plan their position correctly. They must be able to move forward at a charge to strike the oncoming enemy with some momentum. Yet the clash must occur precisely in front of the hidden bowmen, to take advantage of whatever help they could offer.

So the horsemen of the People sat, their elk-dogs fidgeting in the trampled mud. Waiting was the hardest part, Heads Off had always thought. Yet they must remain exactly here and make the enemy come to them, or lose whatever element of surprise their position might furnish when the bowmen struck.

The wait was not long. The milling horsemen out on the plain formed into a semblance of order and faced toward the besieged People. Someone gave a long yell.

Heads Off thought it was the arrogant young chief he had noticed before, but the distance was too great to be sure.

The enemy warriors kicked horses into a frantic gallop and surged forward in an awesome charge.

Good, thought Heads Off. Their horses will be tiring when we strike. They should save them for a final push. Our mounts will be fresh.

It was a vain hope, a slim grasping at straws, he saw in the next moment. The massed might of the charging horsemen was terrifying to see. The falsetto *yip-yip-yip* of the Head Splitters' war cry screamed from a hundred throats.

Heads Off glanced around to see if any of his young warriors might be tempted to run. None appeared to be so inclined. They gripped weapons tightly, ready to move on signal, as the thundering horde pounded down on them.

"*Aiee,*" murmured Long Elk softly to himself.

It was now time to move. Heads Off gently kneed the gray mare Lolita into position and moved forward at a walk. The others fanned out to either side of him, presenting a line of warriors across the narrow neck of the meadow.

There had been a wall of brush and logs. The camp was now protected by a wall of flesh and bone, that of men and of elk-dogs. And, how very fragile that wall appeared, with the overwhelming might of the massed charge bearing down.

The timing must be precise, now. Heads Off touched the mare into a trot. Her ears were forward, eagerly anticipating the excitement of the charge. She had engaged in this sort of activity before. The animal pranced a little. Her rider had often felt that Lolita enjoyed the chase and the shock of the strike as the lance found its mark. Many buffalo had fallen before this team of man and horse, and a few men. It made little difference to the mare. She was straining at the rawhide war bridle when finally Heads Off let her go and voiced the war cry of the People.

The two charging, screaming lines of horsemen approached each other, at almost the exact spot he desired. The Head Splitters were crowding together as they funneled into the neck of the meadow, while the People tried to spread to fill it.

It was perhaps a split second too soon that the bow-men released their first flight of arrows, but it made no difference. The front ranks of the enemy were close, close enough to see the surprise on their faces when the arrows struck among them. Several warriors in the first row were knocked from their mounts. A horse screamed in pain, and another fell heavily, the animal behind col-liding with the rolling body.

Into this confusion charged the Elk-dog warriors of the People. Heads Off had a quick thought of fervent hope that the bowmen would select their targets carefully in the melee. Then he was bearing down on a burly Head Splitter and had no time for such thoughts.

The other was quick and adept. He parried the lance with his shield and swung his war club, but was knocked from his horse by the lance of Standing Bird. Heads Off wheeled and looked for another target. Long Elk had lost or broken his lance, and an enemy horseman charged down on the unprotected youth. Heads Off turned to help him, but the agile young warrior threw himself backward from his horse, somersaulting to land on his feet. He had practiced this maneuver many times, to the amusement of the older warriors. Now it was lifesaving, as the war club of his adversary whistled through the empty space above the horse's withers.

Long Elk ran, bending and twisting, while the mounted Head Splitter pursued him. Heads Off surged forward in a charge and this time his thrust was true. The enemy fell heavily in the mud and lay still.

Heads Off glanced quickly around. A Head Splitter was helping a wounded comrade swing up behind him. Beyond that, another enemy warrior kicked his horse around to retreat. All along the line of the battle, the attackers were withdrawing. Another shower of arrows rattled among them as the bowmen found clear targets again. Several of the young Elk-dog warriors of the People seemed inclined to pursue, but Heads Off called them back.

"Fall back!" he called.

He must not allow them to divide their slim force. They would be unprotected in the open.

"We will have another chance," he reassured the re-turning young men.

32
>> >> >>

The Elk-dog men hastily reassembled in the meadow, to assess the situation. There were three dead, one wounded. Long Elk had recaptured his horse and looked none the worse for his narrow escape.

Several enemy dead lay scattered across the prairie where the action had been heaviest. The bowmen had been the deciding factor, and they had received not one injury. Unfortunately, this element of surprise was now lost. The enemy would be aware of the hidden warriors and their deadly capability.

A rider loped back to the woods, where the women reported no attack at all. Apparently all the Head Splitters, in their comparatively disorganized state, had elected to take part in the grand charge that was to have been the last.

Now, the situation was changed. The enemy was aware that a determined People would not lie down and be killed without a final defense. The Head Splitters would be more cautious about their charge, and would probably attack from the stream and through the woods as well. It had been obvious that there was not much plan in the attack that the People had just turned back. The next strike would be different.

Heads Off wished badly to go to the side of Tall One, but it could not be. He must lead his Elk-dog men in the meadow. Without his leadership he was afraid their youth and inexperience would make them easy prey to the overwhelming force of the enemy.

"*Aiee*, they come again!" Standing Bird pointed.

Heads Off barely had time to swing his horsemen into position before the charge came. They were fewer in number, less than half the strength of the previous charge.

He was puzzled at this turn of events. There had been no time for the planning of the multiple attack he had expected.

The yelling horsemen came closer, and the People began to recognize individuals. Now Heads Off understood. These were the young braggarts who had shouted threats and obscenities at the barrier each day. Furious with the failure of the initial charge, they had mounted their own, probably in defiance of their chiefs' wishes.

The barrage of arrows and spears slowed the enemy charge, almost breaking the thrust of the attack before the countercharge by the Elk-dogs struck. It was only a moment before the Head Splitters were in full flight, again leaving bodies behind on the field.

Heads Off was elated that they had been able to turn the second attack, but was soon sobered. The People had lost two more warriors, and this attack, stopped with relative ease, was not that of the main enemy force. The attack in strength was yet to come.

Time passed slowly for the waiting defenders, and it was near the top of Sun Boy's path when a group of three Head Splitters rode slowly out from their camp toward the defenders.

In the center, flanked by two others, was the young chief Heads Off had noticed before. The three rode at a walk to a place a few hundred paces away and stopped. The leader signed that he wished to talk.

"It is a trick, Heads Off," Long Elk warned.

The chief nodded. "Probably. But we must talk. Come." He beckoned to Standing Bird, then turned to the others. "Watch with care!"

He waved to the bowmen and signed to them also to

be alert, then rode slowly forward. His two young warriors were at his side, alert for any sign of treachery. The two little groups stopped a few paces from each other, suspicious and ready for trouble, but trying to appear relaxed and confident. Heads Off supposed there would be an offer to accept surrender. He had already rejected this in his mind. The possibility of treachery was too likely if the People were to give up their weapons.

"Greetings, my chief," the Head Splitter signed. He was smiling and appeared friendly. "We ask to come and take away our dead."

It was a legitimate request, and took the emissaries of the People by surprise. Heads Off nodded, at the same time thinking rapidly.

"Of course. We will not attack while you take them."

Something was wrong. The request was valid, but seemed inappropriate somehow. How he wished Coyote were at his side. His father-in-law would see through the intricacies of this negotiation.

The enemy chief glanced at the sun. Ah, thought Heads Off, he is thinking about the time. Whatever his scheme, it depends on Sun Boy. This reasoning gave added confidence, and he decided to prolong the encounter a bit. Perhaps he could learn more.

"It is a good day to fight," Heads Off offered pleasantly.

"It is a good day to die!" the other retorted.

"Yes," agreed Heads Off. "Your young men have learned that."

Anger flared on the face of the other. The jibe had struck home, a reference to the lack of organization and control among the Head Splitters. Quickly, the enemy chief regained his composure.

"It is your people who will learn this day," he threatened, yet in a mild and friendly manner. Again, he glanced anxiously at the sun. "Then we may come for our dead?" he questioned, apparently eager to end the interview.

Heads Off nodded, and lifted Lolita's rein to signal the end of the conversation. Boldly and deliberately, he turned his back to the other, attempting to show confidence. He knew Long Elk and Standing Bird would be alert to defend and warn against any overt moves.

A flash of motion caught at the corner of his vision. A man on foot was slipping behind the shoulder of the rocky hill on his left. Now alert to this area, he saw another, bending to hide in the scrubby brush.

Now he saw the reason for the parley.

Normally, the enemy would not have requested to remove bodies until after the battle. To do so now was to use time, to create a distraction, so that warriors could maneuver into position. During the removal of the dead, when the attention of the People was occupied by that activity, enemy warriors on foot would be slipping into position in the woods, behind the hill, and along the stream. When the next attack came, it would be from all quarters at once, not just the frontal charge.

At least, he thought, we can be aware of it. We will not be caught by surprise. The two young horsemen were sent to warn the bowmen, while he himself rode to the woods to warn the defenders there. It gave him another last opportunity to speak to Tall One. He stepped down for a moment for a quick embrace, but realized he must return to the meadow. The girl gave him a quick kiss.

"Remember, the signs are good!"

He smiled and nodded, thinking to himself that of the signs he had seen, none appeared good. He turned Lolita back toward the meadow.

A party of the enemy was lifting their fallen warriors and placing them on the backs of horses they had brought for the purpose. They were singing, he supposed their song of mourning, and his own warriors watched from a distance, fascinated.

"You have told them what we think is to come?" he asked Long Elk.

The other nodded. "We will be ready, Heads Off."

Bowmen were deploying in the scrubby growth of willows along the stream. The Elk-dog men would do without their support at the next charge. The enemy had now correctly determined the weakness of the People. They had simply not enough warriors, even with women and children helping, to defend in so many places at once.

The last of the dead were retrieved, and the funeral party made its way back toward the enemy camp. Now the Head Splitters began to mount, milling around in the characteristic activity that was a preface to their charge. A few began their yipping falsetto war cry, as more horsemen joined the milling throng. If anything, despite the losses by the enemy in the two charges earlier, there seemed to be more horsemen than ever.

A phrase of the death song flitted through the mind of Heads Off for a moment.

". . . today is a good day to die."

He gripped his lance and resolved that the People would give the enemy a day to remember.

As if to echo the phrase of the death song, a new group of horsemen now appeared silhouetted on the hilltop against the western sky. They were in position for a flanking attack when the defenders rode out to meet the charge.

He wondered wryly what White Buffalo might say now, about his signs.

33

>> >> >>

T all One crouched in the dusky shadows of the woods and gripped her bow. The distant song of a bird establishing nesting territory lilted pleasantly in some hidden glade.

The girl glanced continually around the half circle of her vision. Soon there would be shadowy figures of the enemy slipping among the trees. She strained to see, and could imagine movement in the thickets. Abruptly, she shook her head and became more alert to the actual situation. The nesting bird still sang undisturbed. There would be time to prepare, because they would be warned of any approach through the woods when the bird stopped his song.

Tall One looked across the intervening bramble of berry bushes at the hiding place of Antelope Woman. Her friend smiled and signed a question.

"Do you hear the bird?"

Tall One nodded. "It will be our scout," she signed back.

She turned and relayed the information to Big Footed Woman, several paces to her left. The older woman had carefully arranged several heavy throwing sticks on the ground beside her.

Tall One was almost amused. Her mother's skills with the sticks was well-known. There had been much laughter over the way her throwing stick had knocked a Head Splitter off the top of the barricade during the first attack.

Now, Tall One noticed for the first time, her mother had also laid out a stone war club. When the combat became too close for throwing, Big Footed Woman would turn to the hand weapon. Tall One had seen her demonstrate skill with that instrument, as well.

She shuddered a little at the implications of this line of thought. The fighting would become close hand-to-hand conflict as their position of defense was overrun. Tall One would much prefer to use her bow and arrows at a distance. She had always been adept with the bow. As youngsters in the Rabbit Society, she and Antelope Woman had been as accomplished as any of the boys. Her friend could swim like a fish. Tall One herself had been proud of her ability to outrun most of the other children.

Strange, she mused, that her thoughts today would turn to her childhood. So much had happened, so many changes. The coming of the hair-faced stranger, feared at first by the People, but now one of them. Their leader and her own husband, in fact. She smiled to herself. It always gave her a warm, good feeling to think of Heads Off. He was a strong, yet gentle and tender man. It had been heartbreaking to see the Elk-dog band of the People weakening and rotting from within under his leadership. Worst of all, it had not been his fault, she loyally told herself. Under most chiefs, they would have been overrun long ago, possibly even at the time of the Great Battle, several seasons back.

Yes, he had given much to the People. The tribe now had had much food and many robes, with the change in hunting methods. They had become a respected force on the prairie since they learned to hunt with the elk-dog. How unfortunate that his own band, the one now called the Elk-dogs because of the great medicine of her husband, was to be the one to be lost. The other bands would continue to benefit for many lifetimes, but their own, the Elk-dogs, would be absent in the circle.

Tall One glanced up at the leafy arch over them. The massive oaks had dropped their brown leaves, and were well-garmented with new growth. She had always liked

the delicate colors of pink and pale green seen in the
oaks at this time. In fact, this was one of her favorite
moons of the year. She reveled in the warm south breezes,
the damp earthy smell of the woods, and above all, the
greening of the prairie. It was a good day.

"A good day to die . . ."—the phrase from the death
song thrust itself intrusively at her. Tall One had many
regrets at this turn of events. Ordinarily, to die in such a
situation would be no disgrace, if it were done proudly
and well. But there were so many things to think of.

Her small boys. If they were spared, they would be
raised as Head Splitters. Eagle might be old enough to
remember his proud heritage as one of the People, but
Owl certainly could not.

As for herself, Tall One had decided that she would
not be taken alive. It was tempting to imagine that she
might, even though captive, be able secretly to teach the
children of the People their true heritage. She had rejected this. It would be more fitting for the wife of a great
chief to die fighting the enemy. Then the older of the
children in captivity could remember and teach the others this proud bit of their history. She must not allow the
enemy to boast that they had shamed the great Heads
Off by making his woman a slave-wife.

Of course, they would pay dearly for her life, she
thought. Both she and Antelope Woman were well supplied with arrows. When the infighting came too close,
each had also a short buffalo spear. And even beyond that,
the knife at her waist could be used with deadly skill.

If the signs of the medicine man were wrong, and she
was to accompany her husband this day to the Land of
Shadows, she intended to make it an event to be remembered among the People. She must see how many of the
enemy she could start on the journey to their own
shadow-land.

At the thought of the medicine man, she began to
wonder again at the puzzling verdict he had pronounced.
"The signs are good," she had told her husband in parting. Tall One was not deluded into any false sense of
optimism. Her reason told her that the situation was
grim. Perhaps White Buffalo's vision told him only that
the signs were good for a day of honor.

Yes, that must be it, she decided. The Elk-dog band

would go out in an honorable defeat that would be told and retold for many generations. The council fires of both the People and the enemy Head Splitters would hear the tale of valor countless times.

Satisfied as to the meaning of the medicine man's prediction, Tall One settled back to wait. She was pleased, somehow. Now that she understood, she hoped that her own part in the honorable defeat would be deserving of a song. She must strike so many of the enemy that her own deeds would become legend. She counted her arrows again. It was her hope that each one would assist a Head Splitter on his shadowy journey.

Behind her in the camp, she dimly heard a drum establish a cadence. White Buffalo would be in his lodge, chanting a song and casting his medicine stones.

An elk-dog whinnied somewhere, and in the camp another answered. Then she began to hear, in the distance of the open prairie, the ragged sound that was designed to strike terror to the hearts of the defenders. At first it was an isolated staccato *yip-yip-yip*, then joined by others, the sound flowing together and gaining in strength and volume.

She could imagine the attacking warriors swinging to the backs of their elk-dogs. Almost, she could feel the coming tremble of the earth under the hundreds of pounding hooves. Her heart rose in her throat as she thought of her husband and his thin line of Elk-dog warriors bracing to meet the charge. She must be worthy of him.

Tall One gripped her bow tightly and peered expectantly through the shadows. A movement on the right caught her eye, and she turned to look at her friend. Antelope Woman was trying to attract her attention, pointing to the woods ahead.

"The bird has stopped singing," she signed.

34
>> >> >>

Tall One rose to one knee and fitted an arrow to her bowstring. She hoped that no one in the ragged line of women, old men, and youths would give away their positions until necessary. With luck, each of the archers could account for at least one enemy before they were located.

A squirrel began to scold in front of her position, out of sight in the woods. For an instant she wondered how the creature had survived the intense hunting pressure through the winter. A jay flared from the thicket, squawking in alarm.

It seemed an endless length of time before she could see a figure slipping quietly from tree to tree. This man would be a scout, she knew, and it would be much better not to kill him until the main body of enemy warriors were within bowshot.

She watched him carefully. He had not yet located any of the hidden defenders. His line of movement was taking him directly toward the hiding place of Big Footed Woman. Tall One knew that her mother would remain hidden until the last possible moment. She decided that if necessary she could quickly loose an arrow in that direction. She would watch the progress of the man, and let the others watch for the line of warriors that would be following him.

The enemy was carrying a bow at ready, and from his waist dangled the ever-present stone war club. He stepped quietly, eyes shifting from side to side. Once Tall One thought he had looked directly at her, but she held very still and he moved on. In a few more paces he would step almost on top of Big Footed Woman. Tall One made ready to draw her bow.

Suddenly the warrior seemed to see the half-hidden woman. He jumped as if he had been poked with a stick, and with a muffled exclamation swung his bow into position. It was only half drawn, however, when a heavy throwing stick seemed to leap at him.

Big Footed Woman had apparently waited motionless with the weapon already drawn back to throw. When discovered, she flung the club forward with all her strength. As long and as thick as one's arm, the heavy weapon whirled with an audible swishing sound across the few intervening paces. There was a loud crack as it struck the partly drawn bow, and the arrow was diverted harmlessly into the ground. The other end of the still whirling club struck the Head Splitter just above the left eye, and he stumbled to catch his balance. He fumbled for another arrow, then dropped his damaged bow and reached for the war club at his waist.

Before he could free it from its thong, his opponent was upon him. The man was still fumbling for his weapon when another of the woman's sticks, wielded as a club this time, thunked solidly against his head and he collapsed to the ground.

Big Footed Woman snatched up the other throwing stick and darted back to concealment. As if this were a signal, the silence of the woods was broken by the yipping war cry of the attackers. A single arrow reached after the retreating woman, but rattled harmlessly into the bushes.

Tall One turned to see a shifting, dodging line of warriors darting among the trees before her. She drew a quick arrow at a tall warrior and felt the disappointment of failure as the man dodged and the arrow sped harmlessly on. Seeking to take advantage of her weaponless moment, he sprinted forward. In doing so, he became careless, and probably never was aware that Antelope Woman's was the arrow that felled him.

Tall One loosed another shaft at an advancing warrior, and saw him drop to all fours to retreat, plucking from time to time at the feathered shaft through his shoulder.

More and more of the yipping enemy surged forward. Arrows were whistling past her position, and Tall One returned the missiles as fast as she was able. There were several still figures on the ground now. One man, an arm pinned to his side by an arrow, staggered aimlessly about until he fell heavily.

There was a sudden exclamation from Antelope Woman. Tall One glanced that way to see a long gash across the girl's arm turning rapidly scarlet. A burly warrior was rushing forward. Tall One reached for an arrow, but not before the other girl was able to seize her spear. The momentum of the attacker, rather than the skill of the thrust, impaled the surprised Head Splitter. Tall One turned again to her own defense.

In the distance, a woman screamed, and the yipping war cry of the enemy seemed everywhere. Dimly, only half-recognized in her thoughts, was the realization that behind her in the direction of the mounted attack, the din was mounting. Now she could hear and feel the earth tremble from the drumming of unseen hooves as the main charge thundered down.

Nearby, a woman raised her voice in the death song.

> "The grass and the sky go on forever,
> But today is a good day to die."

Others were joining in the song. Tall One saw that she had only two arrows left, and it seemed that an endless number of the enemy were filtering through the woods. She loosed an arrow and reached for the last one, seeking a target.

Her mind was with her husband, at the other point of attack. She realized that she would be able to tell by the sounds of the battle when the enemy charge struck. She listened as the thunder increased in volume and the yipping war cry from a hundred throats grew to a climax.

She heard the steady beat of hooves falter and become ragged as the charge ended in what she knew was the clash. Mixed with the yipping of the enemy was the full-throated war cry of the People. It began in only a few throats, but swelled as other voices joined. Some distance to her left, an aging warrior sprang forward, bellowing the attack in a cracked voice.

Now the yipping falsetto of the attacking horsemen was fading. It was replaced by a rising cry that she recognized as that of the People. From the direction of movement, it seemed ... but *aiee*, that could not be ... her husband and his small handful of warriors were attacking!

The scattered enemy before the defenders in the woods had now stopped to listen, too. There were no more yipping cries, only startled questions tossed back and forth. A warrior turned to retreat, and Tall One loosed her last arrow. Others were retreating, stumbling in their haste, calling to each other.

Some miracle had occurred! What was to have been the final charge and the end of the Elk-dog band, had somehow been turned around.

White Buffalo had been right. The signs were good.

35

>> >> >>

Heads Off had watched the charge form with detachment. It was not despair, but was beyond that. In his own mind, he realized later, he had already accepted the total annihilation of the Elk-dog band. Thus, as the attacking force formed up in the distance, he had become cold and objective. His detachment now allowed him to observe the enemy strategy and evaluate it critically.

This time they were well organized. Warriors on foot, he knew, were moving into position for diversionary attacks from several quarters. It would be up to the bowmen along the stream, the women in the woods, to stop these attacks on their own. The entire force of the horsemen must be used to stem the main charge. And that, he realized, was a hopeless situation.

So, in this, his last battle, he found it amusing in this strange detached way, to observe the enemy tactics. There was one maneuver that he did not quite understand, as the Head Splitters began to mount for the attack. He was puzzled by the horsemen on the hill. He had not noticed them before. In fact, they appeared to be newcomers, just arriving in time for the kill. There was a bit of confusion among them, he thought, some argument and gesturing.

That was a poor position for a flanking attack. He would have placed them across the creek to the east. The stream would slow their charge, but allow a diversionary attack on the weakest flank, and put them behind his poor group of defenders.

The way the new group of horsemen were located, they would actually contribute little to the attack. When they came down from their hilltop they would encounter the fight from nearly the same angle as the main charge. Both would be funneled into the narrow bottleneck where the defenders would meet them. From the People's standpoint, it would make little difference. Either of the enemy groups could probably overrun his handful of warriors.

Still, he was puzzled by the behavior of the group on the hill. They seemed indecisive. There was more arguing and gesturing. Heads Off could not see them well at this distance, and was further handicapped by seeing them only as silhouettes against the bright western sky.

Suddenly he realized the reason for the confusion. For some of it, at least. From where the newcomers stood, they could not be seen by the main camp of the Head Splitters. The shoulder of the hill would intrude on their line of sight. The main group might be completely oblivious to the presence of the others.

Both groups of attackers, in fact, might be unaware of each other. This might account for the indecisiveness on the hill. They could be arguing whether to attack. Still, how could the newcomers fail to see that a battle was beginning? Perhaps they were unsure as to the identity of the attackers. The entire matter became more confusing.

There was no time to contemplate further. The distant enemy were mounted now, the faint yipping war cries beginning to melt together into a chorus of sound designed to terrify. He knew that it would also serve as a signal for the warriors on foot to begin the attack. Then the charge began.

The People had seen this spectacle so many times recently that it seemed commonplace. The Elk-dog warriors moved forward at a walk into line to meet the charge. Heads Off was pleased to see that none faltered. Somewhere at the far end of the line a warrior raised his voice in the death song. The young chief wished for a moment that they wouldn't do that. It seemed so final. In reality, today was to be final, he realized, but still, he hated the admission.

The Head Splitters gained in momentum and volume, the high-pitched *yip-yip* of their attack becoming louder as they approached. There would be no doubt now in the minds of the horsemen on the hill as to the identity of the attackers.

He kneed the gray mare into a trot and the others kept pace. The charging Head Splitters thundered past the shoulder of the hill and began to crowd into the narrowing portion of the meadow. From the corner of his eye, Heads Off was aware that the newcomers on the hill were beginning their charge too. They poured down the slope, lances at the ready, an efficient-appearing band of horsemen. Their charge would be a little late, he noted dully. The first rank of the attacking main force would be well past before the newcomers could join them.

Now the new horsemen began their war cry as they came charging down the slope into the battle. It was a long moment before the reality sank home to Heads Off. The sound that came ringing down the hillside and reverberating against the trees behind him was not the yipping falsetto of the enemy, but the full-throated war cry of the People.

Confused, he reined to a stop to evaluate the changing scene. The enemy charge faltered, too, and they began to mill around in indecision, colliding with each other in disorganized confusion. How could this be, the enemy obviously was thinking, that we are attacked in the middle of an attack? Some of the Head Splitters turned to meet the rush of the new assault, while others made as if to continue the charge. Still others continued to mill about in confusion.

Heads Off was still watching in shocked disbelief. Where had this new force of attackers come from? They were obviously of the People, it could now be seen not only from their war cry, but from their dress and weapons. They charged from the slope and out onto the meadow. The element of surprise was the important factor, perhaps more so than the advantage of momentum and the blow to the unprotected flank of the enemy.

In total number, the People were still outmanned, but were now in a position of tactical advantage. Just before the flanking attack struck, someone identified their new allies.

"It is the Bloods!"

"The Bloods!" The cry went up and down the line, and the People's war cry rose from exultant throats. Heads Off could now plainly see the bright scarlet band across each forehead.

Along the creek, bowmen echoed the full-throated yell. The enemy warriors on foot in the dogwood thickets along the stream saw an unpleasant situation shaping up and began to retreat. After a few parting shots, the bowmen of the People turned and began to run to join the fight in the meadow.

Now the Head Splitters, still confused and disoriented, were being attacked almost simultaneously from both sides, by the Bowstrings from the creek and by the Bloods from the hillside.

Quickly, Heads Off evaluated the rapidly changing scene. Given the terrain and the tactical situation as it now existed, there was only one possible course of action. He lifted his buffalo lance and shouted for the attention of his elk-dog warriors.

The gray mare was plunging with excitement now. He turned her in the general direction of the battle and let her have her head. Without further signal Lolita leaped forward like a great cat, and her rider roared a yell that moved his warriors forward as one.

"Charge!"

36
>> >> >>

Before the Elk-dog warriors fully struck the battle, it was almost over. Head Splitters, unsure and bewildered, were in full retreat, scattering as they ran. Heads Off was unable to strike a single blow with his lance.

It was to be hoped that his warriors would not pursue the retreating enemy out onto the prairie in unprotected positions. They seemed not inclined to do so. A few of the Bloods made a token charge after the retreating enemy, but then returned.

A young Blood warrior approached him at a trot, and reined his horse to a stop. It was Red Dog.

"*Ah-koh*, my chief." He smiled with genuine respect. "It is a good day for a fight."

Heads Off sat, still dumbfounded at the rapid turn of events. He glanced again at the ridge above him and saw a solitary figure still outlined against the sky. There was something familiar about the way the man sat.

"It is Badger." Red Dog spoke at his elbow. "He would not come with us."

Heads Off nodded. The situation now began to make sense. The argument on the hill, the indecisiveness. Red

Dog had assumed command and led the Bloods in their amazing charge, when Badger had refused. The Bloods had followed their new leader. Now Badger sat, rejected and angry, alone.

Someone called out and pointed. A handful of the enemy were climbing the hill, intent on escape. Heads Off recognized the young chief whom he had noticed before. The man seemed to be the leader of the retreating group. He was choosing a good line of escape, seeking higher ground above the conflict. He was a good leader.

At first it appeared that the Head Splitters were not aware of the horseman above them. At what point he was seen was unclear, and mattered little anyway. Their line of flight would bring them in direct contact. The People watched, fascinated.

Above the scattered noise and confusion on the plain below, the intermittent cries and nickers of the elk-dogs, now rose another sound. The solitary figure on the hill was singing the death song of the People. Badger moved his big horse forward to meet the advancing enemy.

The first of the Head Splitters was still off balance at the lip of the hill when Badger struck. The others scattered to climb to the flat top of the ridge at different points. Yet another felt the lance of the young Blood before the rest gained the hilltop. For a few heartbeats there was a flurry of activity as three horsemen closed at once on the lone warrior. Badger had stopped his song now, and fought in silence.

The struggling figures tumbled to the ground for a moment, and then slowly began to rise. The watchers could not see how many remained on the ground, but recognized the young Head Splitter chief as he stepped forward to face them from the rim of the hill. Slowly he lifted a long buffalo lance as if to show it to the People below. Heads Off believed it to be Badger's lance.

With a last defiant yipping cry, the four remaining enemy swung to their horses and departed in the direction of their camp, leading the horses of their comrades and the big black that had been Badger's.

"He was a brave man." Heads Off spoke solemnly to Red Dog.

"Yes, my chief, but sometimes wrong."

Coyote trotted up, grinning through a layer of dust and

sweat. He nodded to the young Blood warrior and spoke to the chief.

"They go!" He pointed out onto the plain.

Though Sun Boy's torch was moving low in the west, the Head Splitters were breaking camp. The first of their column was already forming up to depart over the hill to the south. Even while the People watched, a lodge came down in frantic haste as the inhabitants prepared to retreat.

A thought occurred to Heads Off.

"Where are your women?" he asked Red Dog.

"About two suns north." The other pointed. "They are camped with some Growers. We came to trade, and the Growers told us of this." He spread his hands in an all inclusive gesture around him. "The message had gone out to all the Head Splitters to be here for the kill."

The young man was silent a long moment, then spoke again, hesitantly, and with respect.

"My chief, are we welcome in your camp?"

Heads Off was startled. He had almost forgotten the edict of the Big Council. He was inexperienced in tribal custom, and did not know how matters would stand now.

It was a shock to find the Bloods even alive. The enemy had apparently been so preoccupied with the destruction of the Elk-dog band that they had overlooked the small and vulnerable Blood Society, alone on the prairie.

Now the status of the Bloods was in doubt. Their leader was dead, and it was against him that the Council had ruled. Still, the others had withdrawn from the tribe to follow him.

There seemed little doubt as to their status with the Elk-dog band. There were warm greetings, shouts of recognition, and reaffirmation of friendships. The women, children, and oldsters came straggling from the woods with joyful cries of reunion. A tearful mother embraced her son, whom she had given up for dead, and smudged the embarrassed warrior's crimson paint.

Heads Off had hurriedly taken leave of the activity in the meadow and loped to the woods to find Tall One. She came bounding toward him, nearly knocking him from his horse.

"What happened, my husband? Someone said it is the Bloods?"

He vaulted to the ground and gathered her in his arms.
"The children are safe?"

"Yes, the attack had just begun."

Here and there, a voice lifted in the lamenting wail of
the song of mourning. The People were not without
casualties. Still, that they had survived at all was such an
unexpected triumph that the general atmosphere was
one of jubilation.

Children were brought from their hiding places, and
scattered to find their own families. Crow Woman came
to hand tiny Owl to his mother.

"The signs were good!" she reminded Tall One with a
wrinkled smile.

The day was rapidly drawing to a close. Someone had
already started a large fire in the center of the camp.
There would be a victory celebration like none ever seen.
But first, Heads Off realized, he must call a council.

"Coyote!" he called.

"Yes, my chief, you wish a council?" The little man
had anticipated again.

Heads Off nodded, and knew that the word was probably already spreading. Just now, he felt, he should go and
speak to White Buffalo of his remarkable prediction.

37

》》 》》 》》

As the time for the council drew near, the celebration was already starting. White Buffalo was strutting through the village, resplendent in his paint and finery. He was only too ready to accept the congratulations and to take credit for the astonishing turn of events.

Heads Off wondered if the medicine man himself had actually believed his predictions. From an objective view, it had been a shrewd thing to do. If the band survived it would be remembered that the signs had been favorable, and the strength of White Buffalo's medicine would gain in prestige. If not, it would hardly matter. The Elk-dog band of the People would be dead, along with all memory of the medicine man's favorable prediction.

The young chief had boundless admiration for the ability of the medicine man to manipulate each ensuing situation. Invariably, White Buffalo could maneuver so that his prestige was increased and his medicine made stronger.

Heads Off had once asked his father-in-law about this. Coyote merely shrugged.

"Who knows? White Buffalo is a good medicine man."

In this present instance, Heads Off strongly suspected that, having nothing to lose and all to gain, the old man had simply chosen to give the favorable report. Yet, he had seemed genuinely surprised when he cast the stones. Had that, too, been a part of the charade?

No matter, the young man finally decided. Coyote had summed up the situation nicely.

"White Buffalo is a good medicine man."

Perhaps the entire mystery was encompassed in that one observation. Heads Off shrugged to himself. No matter. He would never know.

Long Elk, Standing Bird, and a few of the Bloods had now returned from a cautious scout of the area. The Head Splitters had really departed for good, it seemed. In their haste, the enemy had left most of the supplies in their abandoned camp. There was even one usable lodge, the scouting party reported, and many lodge poles.

They had quickly gathered all the loose elk-dogs they could. Driving these animals and carrying what supplies of food they were able, the scouts returned just before dark, laughing and singing in triumph.

Now, as the council began to gather, the pleasant smell of cooking fires drifted gently through the camp. There would be much feasting throughout the night. By tradition, the People were accustomed to hunger or plenty, depending on the outcome of the hunt. Now, with food available from the enemy's stores, there was no question as to what should be done. It was time for a feast.

But first, the council. Heads Off passed the pipe, taking care to see that it was offered to Red Dog, as leader of the Bloods. When it was returned after completion of the circle, and replaced in the pipe-case, the chief finally spoke.

"It makes us happy to welcome the return of our brothers, the Bloods. We are one People again!"

He had never heard such a murmur, almost a shout, of approval in council since he had joined the People. It was a few moments before he could be heard again.

"Now," he was finally able to continue, "we must make plans. It is nearly time for the Sun Dance."

More subdued, formal discussion now circled the council fire. There was much to do. There were the dead to care for. Most families wished to salvage lodge poles and whatever else offered from the enemy camp before preparing to travel.

The second sun was chosen as time for departure. It was short notice, but the Elk-dog band would very possibly be late for the Sun Dance now.

The Bloods, it was decided, would comb the area for more elk-dogs while the camp prepared to move. The scouts had seen many other animals on the brief foray just before dark, and they would be badly needed.

As the council drew near a close, Red Dog requested permission to speak.

"My chief," he began, obviously tense, "our hearts are happy for our return, but what of the Big Council?"

There was silence for a long moment, then a subdued whisper in the circle. Many of the People had not foreseen this issue.

"Will we be allowed in the Big Council?"

Now there was a murmur of discussion. The Elk-dog band, owing their lives to the Blood Society, had warmly welcomed them back. However, they now must come face-to-face with the ruling of the Big Council, which would supersede any decisions of individual bands.

Heads Off had placed this problem out of his mind, hesitant to face such a thing. After all, these were the warriors who had defied the Council of Chiefs. They had, in fact, walked out of the Big Council, scorning all tribal authority. This was a far more delicate matter than it appeared.

Individual arguments were starting around the periphery of the circle. Heads Off recognized Coyote's request to speak.

"My chief," the little man spoke with a comic-serious expression, "this is a matter for the Big Council to decide. For now, I am hungry! Let us not use for argument time that could be spent in eating and dancing!"

The council dissolved in good-natured laughter, and someone began to warm and tune a drum by the fire.

It had been a shrewd way to postpone a knotty problem, Heads Off thought. Once again he admired Coyote's skill in council. Even so, he knew the problem was only postponed. He was unsure what measures would be necessary, whether punishment would be forthcoming. He would have to discuss it with Coyote. Ultimately, he supposed, it would be up to the Big Council, what should be done with the Bloods.

He was still concerned, but managed to forget in the excitement of the celebration. The People ate, danced until it seemed they must drop, then ate and rested and started again. Heads Off found that he was the recipient of much honor as leader of the Elk-dog band. He felt that his was no great credit, that mostly good fortune was involved. He looked over to where White Buffalo was accepting homage for his astute predictions and felt somewhat better.

The Seven Hunters and the Real-star were growing pale in the pre-dawn sky before the People shuffled tiredly to their lodges.

Tall One kissed her husband and drew him close, in the warm darkness under their sleeping robes.

"I am very proud, my husband."

"But I did nothing."

"You have led the People to victory. All is good for the future."

In the deep shadows of the woods, *kookooskoos*, the great hunting owl, called to his mate.

Heads Off snuggled closer and relaxed, more content than for many moons. White Buffalo had been right, he decided. The signs were good.

38

›› ›› ››

Sun Boy's torch rose next morning on a band of weary but enthusiastic People. Preparations for departure were already under way. The wailing lament of the Mourning Song hovered over the camp, even as preparations proceeded. This was always a tense and jarring experience for Heads Off. The People said goodbye noisily, with wives and mothers of the deceased smearing themselves with dirt and ashes, sometimes continuing the wailing for several days. One young wife gashed her forearms deeply with her flint knife. Blood mingled with dust and tears as she wrapped the body of her husband for burial.

Heads Off wandered through the camp, attempting to say a few words to each bereaved family. He felt clumsy about it, but it would be expected of him, as leader, that he acknowledge each loss in person.

He encountered Frog Woman, the mother of Badger. The Bloods had brought the young man's body from the hill, and the old woman was engaged in the mourning ritual. She had no one else, Heads Off reminded himself. Her husband was dead, and she existed only with the help of her brother's family. How difficult this past year must have been for her. The young chief was embarrassed that he had not realized this before. What could one say?

"I am sorry, Mother." He placed his hand on her shoulder.

The old woman gave no sign that she was even aware of his presence. She only continued to rock back and forth, wailing the Mourning Song. Heads Off walked slowly away, uncomfortable over the episode. But what could he have said or done?

Coyote fell in beside him, observing his discomfiture.

"It is good, Heads Off. Frog Woman only wishes to be alone."

Yes, Heads Off finally realized. The woman has not only lost her son, but she must know that he was nearly the cause of the death of the entire band. Hers was not a happy lot. Heads Off was almost tempted to turn back, to try to let her know that he understood, but decided against it.

A large party moved out to the abandoned enemy camp for salvage, with a few mounted warriors providing security. Another group of the Elk-dog warriors scattered over the prairie, gathering all possible horses. Some animals had been abandoned, others had escaped from the Head Splitters in the confusion, and still others had become riderless when their warriors were unseated in battle. Several were found still wearing skin saddle pads and trailing broken reins. All these animals were gathered and herded into the protected meadow next to the camp, where young men maintained constant watch to prevent strays.

Shortly after the overhead portion of Sun Boy's journey, all the captured horses were herded together, and the People assembled. Coyote had made suggestions in private to his son-in-law.

"Each family will choose an elk-dog until all are gone," Heads Off announced. "Those who have none come first."

One family at a time, the People moved forward, looked over the available animals, and made their choices. As soon as everyone had at least one animal, the sequence began again, until each horse was the property of someone.

The crowd scattered, some to try out their new acquisitions, some to barter, but many simply to prepare for the move. It would be difficult to assemble and pack each family's belongings by the next sunrise, but it was absolutely necessary.

Already it was well into the Moon of Growing. The Elk-dog band would arrive late for the Sun Dance. It would, in fact, be necessary to send a messenger to announce their impending arrival, but that could come later, when the band was nearer their destination. It would take many suns to reach the Salt River, the appointed site for the Sun Dance.

Closer at hand, they must pause in travel to join the wives and families of the Blood Society, now two suns away. The Growers with whom they were camped lived almost in the line of march, and it would be little trouble to detour in that direction.

Heads Off had considered for a moment sending the Bloods to bring their families to join the band as they traveled. He rejected that plan. It was too risky to divide his force again. The Head Splitters, smarting from defeat, would be unpredictable and dangerous.

The People were moving next morning before full daylight, packing and stowing goods in their rawhide carriers. There were enough elk-dogs to carry the depleted possessions of the band, and to drag all the extra lodge poles salvaged from the enemy. Since most of the range of the People was nearly devoid of timber, good lodge poles could be prized possessions. They could be kept until enough skins for new lodge covers were available.

Heads Off rode to the rim of the hill to watch the caravan move out. In the lead were Long Elk and Red Dog, followed by the first of the family units, pulling their lodge cover on a poledrag. It was a perfectly orderly exit, leaving behind the usual debris of a campsite. It appeared, however, that there was somewhat less remaining trash than usual. The People were in no position to throw away a pair of worn-out moccasins or a tattered garment. This year they would be worn.

He looked across the tops of the oaks in the woods below him, and at the pleasantly sparkling stream. How close this place had come to being the final campsite for them all. He had never expected to watch again the straggling column move across the prairie to their next camp.

This would be a place important in the history of the People. Already he had heard the site called "Bloods' River" by someone, in recognition of the amazing charge that had turned certain defeat into victory.

White Buffalo was already planning the pictograph for the Story Skins, he had told the chief. It would show horses impaling themselves on a barrier of spears, and Blood warriors charging from the hill to strike the enemy. It would be a magnificent thing to depict. This would be known in the future, the medicine man said, as "the year we ate elk-dogs."

And that, Heads Off reminded himself, would be considerably better than "the year the Elk-dog band was wiped out."

He lifted the reins and touched the mare gently forward to rejoin the band.

39
›› ›› ››

T hree of the Bloods had ridden ahead to carry the news to the families at the Growers' village. It was found that they had already heard the news of the battle. The prairie grapevine was swift.

A small band of retreating Head Splitters had stopped to trade for supplies, and had told the story to the Growers. They believed that they had been attacked by the entire tribe of the People, at least by several bands. They recounted the charge from the hill, and that from the camp, and stated that they had been forced to retreat because they were outnumbered.

The Growers were noncommittal. They traded with all other tribes, and their somewhat precarious existence depended on the goodwill of all the hunting groups. Some black glances were thrown toward the families of the Bloods by the Head Splitters, but no overt action was taken. By tradition, one must not attack an enemy or his family or possessions while they are guests of a friendly tribe. To do so would be the worst sort of an affront to their hosts, the Growers. The Bloods' families were quite safe.

Their presence, however, did result in the early departure of the Head Splitters. They had no desire to be in the area when the People came back for their families.

The wives of the Bloods, meanwhile, were almost frantic with worry. They knew there would surely have been casualties. Which of them would have lost a husband or brother? They could only wait, and try to keep busy until they received word. They gathered in groups of three or four, and in tense voices talked about almost anything else to distract them.

The circumstances of the men's departure had been rather unsettling. There had been arguing and dissension. Many of the Bloods had long since realized what most of the wives already knew. To leave the tribe to follow Badger had been a very foolish thing. It was pure good fortune that the little band had not encountered the enemy and been annihilated.

They had temporarily camped to trade with the village of Growers when rumors began to trickle in telling of a coming battle. The Elk-dog band of the People, it was said, were under attack by the Head Splitters, and were about to be overrun.

Most of the Bloods were eager to join the fight, but their leader dissented. Badger, still smarting from the humiliation of the Big Council, smoldered with resentment. He refused to consider such a move, pointing out that the Bloods were no longer a part of the People. If Heads Off and his band were in trouble, so be it. That was the problem of Heads Off, not of the Bloods.

Perhaps it was Badger's repeated references to the young hair-faced chief that began to turn the tide of opinion. All the young warriors present had been taught by Heads Off, and respected his elk-dog medicine. He had been hard, but fair, and none could hold any animosity toward him as their teacher.

When Red Dog finally announced that he was going, nearly every warrior joined him. Badger ranted and swore, at first forbidding anyone to go. Then, seeing he could not prevent it, he eventually joined the war party, all the while advising, complaining, and threatening.

That was the situation when the women had last seen them. It had been apparent that Badger's leadership was slipping, and that an uneasy feeling permeated the Bloods that perhaps their leader's position had not been logical from the first. There were certainly many who deplored the killing of Sees Far, even though it may have been justified.

So, the waiting women at the village of the Growers had many unanswered questions. They did not know whether their men had taken part in the battle. They were forced to assume so because of the Head Splitters' description of great numbers, but how many of them had participated? Had the band split yet again?

With great relief they saw three of their warriors ride in the following evening.

"Badger and Heron are dead," Red Dog told the waiting women. "The rest will be here tomorrow."

The wife of Badger now began the Mourning Song, joined in sympathy by some of the other women. Heron, a lanky youth from the Mountain band, had had no relatives among the Bloods.

"Are there wounded?" a girl asked timidly.

Red Dog nodded. "Yes, but not badly." Quickly he recounted the story.

"*Aiee*," exclaimed a pregnant young woman. "Our men are with the Elk-dog band? Are we able to return to the People?"

"We do not know," answered Red Dog seriously. "The Elk-dog band has made us welcome, but it must come before the Big Council."

In the minds of most, this seemed a more important concern than the loss of their leader. Badger had become so irrational at times that there were those who privately felt a great sense of relief at his demise.

"Then we will go the Sun Dance?" someone was asking.

Red Dog nodded. "We must be ready to move. The Elk-dog band will be here tomorrow."

The group scattered to begin preparations for the journey. The prospect was a happy one. A chance to see friends and relatives again, even temporarily, was a great lift to the spirit.

Red Dog made his way to his own lodge, where he and his young wife talked at great length. He was excited and optimistic. He was somewhat uneasy about the Big Council, but Red Dog had a better feeling than at any time since they left the Sun Dance last year.

40
» » »

The women of the Bloods welcomed their relatives of the Elk-dog band next evening with a feast that would be long remembered. Their food was in good supply, and they had just been trading with the Growers. Cooking had proceeded through the day, even while the preparations to depart continued.

The reunion, feast, and dance celebration became so exuberant that the Growers shook their heads in despair at the proceedings. Anxious mothers of the village cautioned their children against contact with the strange visitors and their well-known excesses.

This bothered the People not at all. There was a sense of reunion and homecoming, both on the part of the Bloods and that of the main Elk-dog band. Forgotten for the moment, in the happiness of the day, was the fact that the Big Council might easily refuse to lift the banishment. With their characteristic live-for-today philosophy, the People seemed unconcerned.

But Heads Off was concerned, increasingly so in the coming days as they traveled toward the Salt River. He sought out Coyote for advice and the two walked together, a little apart from the main column.

"What will the Big Council do?"

Coyote shrugged. "It will matter much what the Real-chief says. Most of the chiefs will vote with him."

"What do you think Many Robes will say?"

"I do not know, Heads Off. Many Robes was very angry over the death of Sees Far. But that was mainly against Badger."

The two walked in silence for a long time. An orange-winged grasshopper clacked into flight in front of them and fluttered to a new resting place several paces ahead. As the insect folded its bright wings and melted again into its dusty gray invisibility, Coyote spoke again.

"Maybe you should ask him."

"You mean, before the Big Council?"

Coyote nodded. "Before we get there, maybe. You could go on ahead."

The idea seemed good. They discussed it at greater length, and made some tentative plans. A few suns before their arrival, Heads Off and one or two others would ride ahead. This would serve both to announce their coming and to allow time to consult the Real-chief.

Heads Off would have chosen Coyote and Red Dog to go with him, but the little man dissuaded him.

"No, Heads Off. I do not wish to shake my bones on an elk-dog. You will wish to travel fast and hard. My elk-dog medicine is not as strong as yours." He rubbed his rump ruefully, indicating that he considered the strength of his anatomy as well as that of his medicine.

They talked long of Red Dog. He would make a good impression on the Real-chief, would undoubtedly strengthen their position, but it was risky. Would his presence seem too presumptive? It would never do to alienate Many Robes even before he had time to consider the matter.

In the end it was decided not to allow any of the Bloods near the Sun Dance encampment until after Heads Off had talked with the Real-chief. Long Elk and Standing Bird would accompany Heads Off. After the interview, if it appeared that there was a great deal of animosity toward the Bloods, one of the young men could ride back to carry the message. Then the Bloods could decide whether to come in at all.

Red Dog was taken into the confidence of the chief, and agreed that the plan seemed good.

When the caravan reached a point that was said to be about five suns from the Salt River site for the Sun Dance, Heads Off and his young warriors began their mission.

Heads Off embraced his wife warmly. They had seldom been apart, and he regretted having to leave her now.

"Think of me sometimes," he teased. "I will see you soon!"

Their journey to the Sun Dance site was pleasant. The prairie was green and fresh in the Moon of Roses. Buffalo and antelope dotted the distant hills, and the spicy smell of the grassland with its assorted flowers in full bloom was exhilarating.

In the morning of the third sun they saw ahead the smoke of a large camp, and by halfway through the day could see the first of the lodges. There was always the feeling of excitement at the annual gathering, like the atmosphere at a country fair in the land of Heads Off's childhood. People walked, ran or moved about, called to each other, sang, or in general seemed to be enjoying each other. Dogs barked.

A group of riders swung out to meet them at a hard gallop, showing off their skills with the elk-dogs as they escorted the newcomers in.

Many Robes watched them come, from his comfortable position against his willow backrest. He was delighted to see them. He had had grave doubts about the ability of the Elk-dog band to survive when he saw so many of the younger warriors leave to follow that troublemaker. What was his name? Woodchuck or some such . . . Badger, that was it. There was a bad one, thought Many Robes.

The three men of the Elk-dog band rode up and dismounted to pay their respects. After the amenities, their hair-faced leader spoke.

"May I speak with you, my chief?"

The two young warriors with him slipped discreetly away.

Many Robes nodded, wondering what the problem was.

Heads Off looked thin, and somewhat worried. It could not have been an easy year for him. Then there were the rumors that had filtered to the ears of the Real-chief. Tales of a battle with the Head Splitters, a big battle.

If Heads Off is here, thought the Real-chief, he must have defeated the enemy. Then what could be his problem? Many Robes half-closed his eyes and leaned back. He would learn in a moment.

"My chief will remember," Heads Off began hesitantly, "that many of our young men left the People to follow Badger, who was banished by the Big Council."

The Real-chief nodded, blowing a fragrant wisp of smoke from his pipe. He said nothing.

"Those young men have come back to us," Heads Off continued.

The eyes of the Real-chief widened perceptibly. This could be a big problem, if the Elk-dog band had accepted the miscreants back against the edict of the Council. There must be more.

"We were about to be overrun by the Head Splitters, and they entered the fight."

There was no change on the face of the stoic Many Robes.

"Badger is dead," blurted Heads Off, now desperately looking for some small thing to break the calm composure of the other.

Inwardly, Many Robes relaxed. If that were the case, if the troublemaker was gone, then things could be handled. He closed his eyes.

"Tell me the whole story, Heads Off."

Rapidly, Heads Off sketched in the events of the past year. By the time he described the charge of the Bloods down the slope to strike the enemy's flank, Many Robes was sitting forward, excited.

"And who led them?"

"Red Dog, my chief. Badger had refused, and Red Dog took over leadership of the Bloods."

Many Robes nodded, pleased. That young man would make a great leader.

"Tell me, Heads Off. Is it not true that the Council expelled Badger for killing one of your band?"

"Yes, my chief."

"No others were sent away? They only followed him?"

Heads Off nodded.

Many Robes spread his hands in a gesture of resignation. "Then, where is your problem? Some of your young warriors went their own way for a season, and now they are back. There is nothing wrong with a new warrior society. Your elk-dog men," the old chief smiled amiably, "started a new group."

It was a long speech for Many Robes, and he paused for a little. Heads Off waited.

"When you come to the Council," the Real-chief continued, his tone confidential, "bring your Blood Society in with the others, and say nothing of any problem. I think no one will question it."

Heads Off was elated. It was so simple, now that he had the assurance of the Real-chief. Yes, the Bloods had been on their own for a season, and were now welcomed back. They had returned at a very fortunate time, and had turned the day for the Elk-dog band.

He located Long Elk and Standing Bird, and rapidly sketched in the details of his conversation with the Real-chief.

"Go back to the Elk-dogs," he directed. "Tell Coyote and Red Dog what I have told you. I wish to see Red Dog as soon as he can get here."

Three suns later, as darkness fell, the People gathered for the Big Council. Red Dog led his Bloods into the circle to take their places, well ahead of the arrival of the chiefs. He sat next to Standing Bird, by prearranged plan. At length they were joined by Heads Off.

Many Robes entered with dignity and the Big Council began.

The pipe ceremony progressed, and it was soon time for the chiefs to speak. Each in turn rose to tell of events in his own band.

First, Black Beaver of the Mountain band spoke. It had been a good winter with much game. They had seen no enemies.

"I am White Bear, of the Red Rocks," stated the next chief. "Ours, too, has been a good year." He sketched in a few details.

Next in the circle was the Elk-dog band. Heads Off

rose, hands moist with tension. His elk-dog medicine glinted against his buckskin shirt.

"I am Heads Off, chief of the Elk-dog band," he announced formally. "My brothers, ours has been a very big year."

About the Author
>> >> >>

DON COLDSMITH was born in Iola, Kansas, in 1926. He served as a World War II combat medic in the South Pacific and returned to his native state where he graduated from Baker University in 1949 and received his M.D. from the University of Kansas in 1958. He worked at several jobs before entering medical school: he was a YMCA group counselor, a gunsmith, a taxidermist, and, for a short time, a Congregational preacher. In addition to his private medical practice, Dr. Coldsmith is a staff physician at Emporia State University's Health Center, teaches in the English Department, and is active as a freelance writer, lecturer, and rancher. He and his wife of 26 years, Edna, have raised five daughters.

Dr. Coldsmith produced the first ten novels in "The Spanish Bit Saga" in a five-year period; he writes and revises the stories first in his head, then in longhand. From this manuscript he reads aloud to his wife, whom he calls his "chief editor." Finally the finished version is skillfully typed by his longtime office receptionist.

Of his decision to create, or re-create, the world of the Plains Indian in the 16th and 17th centuries, the author says: "There has been very little written about this time period. I wanted also to portray these Native Americans as human beings, rather than as stereotyped 'Indians.' That word does not appear anywhere in the series—for a reason. As I have researched the time and place, the indigenous cultures, it's been a truly inspiring experience for me."